"Just who are you...
"Find out," the Executioner said.

Kriplin raised the gun. He took a perforated silencer from his pocket and clicked it into position over the Walther's barrel.

"I am sorry about this," he told Bolan with genuine regret in his voice. "But you must see that I have no choice. I am sure you understand that I cannot afford to leave you here alive. I will make it quick."

The long holed tube lined up with Bolan's forehead. Kriplin's forefinger flexed around the trigger.

The sound of the shot was deafening....

MACK BOLAN
The Executioner

DON PENDLETON's EXECUTIONER
MACK BOLAN
Ice Cold Kill

A GOLD EAGLE BOOK FROM

TORONTO · NEW YORK · LONDON · PARIS
AMSTERDAM · STOCKHOLM · HAMBURG
ATHENS · MILAN · TOKYO · SYDNEY

First edition October 1984

ISBN 0-373-61070-X

Special thanks and acknowledgment to
Peter Leslie for his contributions to this work.

Printed in Canada

Success is the child of audacity.
                              —*Benjamin Disraeli*

Let no one mistake duty for foolhardiness.
This war chose me, therefore I feel I must
do what's right. And audacity is inherent in
my quest for justice.
                              —*Mack Bolan*

To the memory of Constable Yvonne Fletcher,
a policewoman, who was cut down in cold blood
by gunfire from the Libyan embassy on April 17, 1984,
in London, England. God rest her soul.

1

Before Mack Bolan was even halfway across the plowed strip that separated the two lines of wire fencing, the frontier guards opened up with a murderous hail of firepower.

Muzzle-flashes split the moonless winter night as Kalashnikov AKMs on full-auto sprayed lead from the watchtower on the Soviet side of the border. Over the blazing clamor of the guns Bolan could hear the 7.62mm slugs thunking into the frozen earth around him.

The Executioner flung himself to the ground, cursing. He had not figured on this lethal surprise. A secret crossing had been fixed for tonight with bribes paid and special cover arrangements organized. But judging by the blistering volley deployed from that tower, someone sure as hell had changed the plans.

Without telling the big guy.

Bolan quickly considered his predicament.

He had been crossed up somewhere along the line, sure, but there was no more time to worry about it now.

Facedown along one of the furrows, in the few seconds it took for the 30-round magazines to exhaust themselves, Bolan sized up the situation. The wire behind him was a simple barbed entanglement. No sweat for the Romanian Gypsies who had been paid to cut it before he went through. But a fifteen-foot chain link fence, maybe electrified, barred the Russian side of the strip.

That figured. No comrades were lining up to leave Romania for the socialist paradise to the north. But there were many dissidents anxious to flee the Soviet Union, and that chain link fence was designed to keep them in.

And to keep guys like Bolan out.

His mission was to get in, then out again with one of the folks who wanted to leave.

Two points remained in Bolan's favor. The place he had chosen for his clandestine entry was a desolate area sixty-five hundred feet up in the Carpathian Mountains. Because Soviet security was less strict here than it was along the borders where Russia faced the West directly, the watchtowers were spaced far apart. But more important, the searchlights were not automated so the plowed strip wasn't swept continuously throughout the hours of darkness.

An additional advantage was that in such a deserted area the guards were armed with the older AKMs rather than the new Kalashnikov AK-74—an autorifle with a muzzle brake that eliminated recoil and climb, tripling the weapon's effectiveness and accuracy.

Bolan stared into the night, eyes straining to pierce the blackness. The winter moon would not rise for another two hours. Even then drifting cloud banks that were erasing whole constellations would minimize the light. He glanced at the luminous dial of his digital watch. He still had thirty-nine minutes before the rendezvous with Schelgatseff.

The Executioner weighed the chances. The shooting had stopped. If he could gain the fence in the seconds before they reloaded their AKMs and activated the searchlight at the base of the tower, he might still make the meeting with his contact. The plowed strip sloped steeply down toward the Soviet side. The watchtower stood twenty feet high and he was roughly eighty yards away. The next tower was a quarter of a mile farther along the ridge. The guards there would be holding their fire until the searchlight illuminated a target.

Bolan heard a shouted command from the tower ahead, boots pounding on an iron ladder, a rattle of metal as the curved, pressed-steel magazines were slammed into place. They would have infrared night sights, for sure. Bolan rose to his feet.

He was wearing a skintight blacksuit over lined neoprene inners designed to keep out the cold. Two eyeholes pierced the black woolen mask covering his face and head, and there was a single Slepoy stun grenade in a pocket on his hip. A short-barreled .357 Model 19 Combat Magnum hung in a loop from his gloved wrist. The only other thing he carried was a long, thin pole made of feather-light fiberglass.

In the instant before the AKMs opened fire again, he translated decision into action. There had never been any question of going back. Orders were to penetrate to the far side of the fence. Blown or not, that was where Bolan was going because the orders were his own.

The Kalashnikovs spit flame, momentarily printing the watchtower's girders against the night. Bolan raced toward them, weaving left and right as his feet pounded the iron-hard frosted furrows.

Red, orange, then blinding white, the searchlight blazed to life. From the farther tower another dazzling beam dissolved the darkness.

Tiger-striped with black shadow, the frozen earth resisted as Bolan planted the tip of the pole in the last groove before the fence.

Three weeks' intensive training under a former Olympic pole vault champion paid dividends now. Besides, the big soldier was an athlete in his own right. Years of fighting in the hellzone under any number of adverse conditions had honed his physique to a hard, fine-tuned machine. The fiberglass rod bowed under his weight as he launched himself off the ground. For one heartbeat he hung motionless in midair in the fetal position. Then Bolan summoned his powerful arm and shoulder muscles to thrust himself away from the pole, kicking out his legs at the same time as he powered himself over the top of the fence into Soviet airspace.

He landed the way he had learned as a jumper in Nam, arms folded, head bent, knees drawn up, hitting the frozen ground hard, rolling forward, the breath slammed from his body. Then he was up, darting for a line of scrub behind the tower, the freezing air scything into his lungs as the searchlights swiveled to chase him into Russian territory.

Bolan hid behind a bush, gulping oxygen as he considered his next move.

He was in. But it was only the beginning.

Once the crossing was no longer a secret, Bolan realized he had to leave the impression of someone getting *out*. Chances were the Russians would be fooled long enough for him to leave the area.

The ridges and furrows of frost-hardened earth showed few marks, even with a big man running. And those that he had left—because of special frames clamped to the soles of his boots—would point to a fugitive speeding toward Romania rather than away from it. The cut wire would be the clincher. But if the ruse was to be successful there must be no witnesses.

He knew he had to dispose of the guards in both towers, then vanish into the darkness before soldiers from posts farther along the line, alerted by the firing, dashed to the scene.

Unless the Russian gunners took him out first.

But plans, Bolan thought grimly, however carefully organized, do not always work out.

Bolan wore the minimum of clothing, carried only necessary arms, for a particular reason: because of the sensitivity of this mission, there had to be no whisper of a trace that a stranger from the West had penetrated the region.

Phosphorus capsules sewn into the suit would cause the material to self-destruct once Bolan was through with it. The grenade was Russian and the gun, although it was a Smith & Wesson design, had been manufactured under license in the Far East.

There were six rounds in the cylinder and that was it. No clips to mar the slickness of the fighting suit, no spent cartridge cases, no clues to tempt a KGB investigator.

Everything Bolan would need while he was in Soviet Russia—clothes, ID, money, cover documents, a vehicle—would be waiting for him at the rendezvous with Schelgatseff half a mile from the border.

For the moment, however, the mission had reduced itself to a problem of mathematics. Bolan had six shots; there were twelve men to deal with; half a dozen in each tower. The equation was therefore simple. And if it was going to work, the six guards in the nearest tower would have to be zapped without mistake. Then Bolan could commandeer one of their AKMs to take care of the men from the other lookout. Bolan knew his aim had to be true. A single mistake or wasted round and he would buy it in that wintry wasteland. Those men were primed to kill. That last thought fired him into action.

The Executioner came out of the bushes running. The searchlight was not far enough around yet to spotlight him. The first shot from the Model 19 picked a guard from the tower and dropped him to earth with a third eye glistening in the reflected light.

Bolan fired again in a two-handed shooting stance to steady the weight of the two-pound Magnum.

Wood splintered and the guardrail collapsed as

another soldier plummeted from the watchtower into oblivion.

Bolan was back in the bushes before the body hit the ground. There were still two guys up there ready to issue him a one-way ticket on the same flight with the third clip in their AKMs. Two bursts chattered as they fired blindly into the scrub.

The remaining pair were operating the searchlight. As the beam steadied on the foliage, one of them fouled up. He was not quick enough stepping out of the way.

For a fraction of a second he was silhouetted against the dazzling lens. The Magnum roared a third time.

The bullet struck the rim of the 100cm searchlight and screeched into the night without breaking the glass. A red spray misted the lens and turned the beam momentarily rose-colored. The soldier fell. Then the searing heat from the 500,000 candlepower arcs dried and blackened the blood until it crisped and dropped away. The light turned white again. Bolan sacrificed his fourth round, firing through wisps of steam and a faint odor of roasting meat to kill the beam.

The fading glow of the element had not completely died and glass was still falling from the frame when he reached the other man.

The soldier's AKM had been slung while he operated the light. In the sudden dark Bolan leaped at the great-coated figure with the Magnum reversed. The Executioner's right arm flailed and the butt struck bone. The Russian grunted and half fell against the big guy.

Bolan groped frantically for a hold. The guard was half out on his feet but he was heavy and he was tough. Bolan gasped as an elbow hammered his thinly clad solar plexus. The edge of his combat-hardened hand sliced down to target on the Russian's throat. Roaring in agony, he tried to grapple Bolan in a bear hug, but Bolan sidestepped and wedged a forearm beneath the man's jaw and kneed his spine. On the frozen ground the struggle terminated with a loud, dull crack. Bolan snatched the sentry's AKM, sprang upright and raced for the tower.

The farther searchlight was on full traverse now, but it had been mounted to monitor the plowed strip, and scrub straggling over the bare ridge between the two towers masked the beam so that the area below Bolan's tower was illuminated only with reflected light.

The two remaining men, crouched on the platform of the tower, were clearer targets than Bolan moving among the bushes. He thumbed the AKM to auto and triggered a couple of short bursts.

Scratch two more soldiers.

Bolan sprinted for the ladder. As he climbed he could hear shouting from the crew of the other tower. Over the broken rail he discerned four figures running, about ninety yards away. They were holding their AKMs in port position. Two soldiers remained at the second tower to work the light.

One of the approaching guards bellowed a question. Bolan had better than a working knowledge of Russian: an earlier immersion course at a U.S. language factory had just been updated by three weeks of saturation work with Russian speakers in Paris.

"This way," he called in reply. "Down among the bushes. Two or three of them, trying to break out."

"How many of you operative?"

"Just two. Bastards picked off the searchlighters and a couple more."

"Very well. Cover us and we'll handle them," the Russian shouted. He waved his men toward the bushes behind the tower.

Bolan crawled across the platform and lifted another Kalashnikov from one of the dead guards. When the four men below were near enough, he shot them down.

He felt no remorse. The unit policing this sector of the frontier, he knew, was fresh back from the occupation force in Afghanistan, where they had been waging chemical warfare against tribesmen armed with nineteenth-century muskets.

Only two guards now remained at the other tower. And it was clear that they were already wise to the fact that someone was playing hell with the border defenses.

Bolan descended the ladder and started running toward the other tower. When he was two hundred yards away, still grasping the Magnum and an AKM, he heard the screech of a field telephone being wound and a jabber of excited voices. Bolan guessed they were calling the next tower down the line.

He was eighty yards nearer when the man not using the phone opened fire. Bolan dropped out of sight behind a rock outcrop, felt slugs whisper past his head. Granite chips stung his cheek. He glanced at his watch. Less than a half hour to make the date with Schelgatseff.

The crewless searchlight was immobile. Bolan wormed his way around the outcrop and rose to his knees in a pool of shadow. The man with the gun was visible, a blur leaning over the rail above the light. As Bolan watched, the second guard slammed down the phone and joined him.

Bolan slid the Slepoy grenade from its pocket, drew the ring and tossed the explosive. Light from the searchlight beam was briefly eclipsed by a livid flash as the thunderclap detonation cracked out below the rail.

Bolan sped through the smoke and took the steps three at a time. The grenade allowed him between six and eight seconds before the enemy recovered from its stunning blast. But he had underestimated the roughness of the terrain and the guards were already staggering to their feet by the time he made the top of the ladder.

One ran at him while the other groped, coughing, for

his gun. The running man kicked viciously at Bolan's face. Bolan rode the blow as the steel toe cap of the Russian's boot thudded against his cheekbone, but the savage impact toppled him backward.

He fell from the ladder, grabbing the guard's foot and twisting as he dropped.

The man flew over his head and crashed heavily to the ground twenty feet below. Bolan hit the rungs twice, bounced and landed, panting, on his hands and knees. His body felt as though it had been flattened by a truck and his heart was thumping, but there was no damage. The guard was not so lucky. He lay groaning with one leg doubled beneath him and his head at an impossible angle. Bolan guessed his back was broken. He helped the guy on his way with the fifth shot from the Magnum.

Flame belched from the watchtower, stabbing through the smoke as the last guard's AKM thundered. Bolan dived for the shelter of the tower to escape the deadly hail of slugs.

He had lost his AKM when he fell from the ladder. Now he looked up at the wooden underside of the tower's floor. The illumination was faint behind the searchlight. He had one shot left in the Magnum's chamber.

He waited, hearing distant shouts from farther along the frontier. In the first tower a telephone was shrilling. Immediately above him a hesitant scrape of feet. Bolan raised the gun, listened again and fired.

A cry up there and a stumbling thump.

The slug had pierced the floorboards, scored the guard's thigh and tunneled through genitals and pelvic girdle to the belly, Bolan discovered when he swarmed back up the ladder. The guy lay in a spreading scarlet pool and there was blood seeping from a corner of his mouth.

Bolan picked up the AKM and emptied the rest of the magazine over the wire, as though gunning for someone on the way to Romania. Then he slid down the ladder, recovered the gun he had dropped and sprinted back to the spot where he had vaulted the fence. Here he exhausted a second magazine, firing into the plowed earth of the strip.

There were high-explosive fragmentation grenades hooked to the belt of a dead guard lying beside the shattered searchlight. Bolan pulled the pin and tossed the HE against the chain links near his entry point.

The fence buckled and sagged, wire snapping with the force of the blast.

But there was no blue flash from a shorted power line. The fence had not been electrified after all.

Bolan ripped two floorboards from the watchtower and threw them down, one sloping up against the savaged fence, the other on the far side near his abandoned pole.

Let the Russians figure out how one escaper had blown the fence and walked over with the help of planks.

Bolan heard approaching voices now from the Romanian side of the strip, demanding what the hell was going on. Bolan left them to it.

On the far side of the scrub, a forest trail snaked downhill through pines and fir trees. It was along this rutted track, Bolan knew, that Red Army trucks from a base camp in the valley below ferried up replacements to spell the guys on frontier detail.

And reinforcements in case of trouble.

Already he could hear the whine of engines as heavy military vehicles labored up the grade toward the sounds of shooting.

Bolan flung the empty Model 19 over the fence, left

the Kalashnikovs where they lay and took off. He was tempted to take one with him but he had to resist. None of the frontier guards' equipment must be missing, and any foreign arms must point toward an escape if he was to gain the respite he so urgently needed.

He jogged easily downhill along the forest trail as the bewildered voices faded behind him. When he saw the lights of the approaching convoy through the treetops below, he left the track and kept to the woods.

It was dark, damp and cold in there. Between the interlaced branches he could see the surrounding peaks were dusted with snow, showing pale in the occasional starlight. But he knew every inch of the terrain like the back of his hand.

Almost a month's study of photo blowups and a sand-table model constructed from satellite pictures had left him confident that he could have found his way blindfolded to the disused quarry where Schelgatseff was waiting for him.

This sector of the frontier near the headwaters of the Cheremosh River, ran between the villages of Moldovita in Romania, and Seletin, five miles away on the Soviet side of the border. Bolan was to follow the river down as far as Chernovtsy and then leave the valley and make his way to Khotin on the Dniester. From there his route continued east until the river ran out into the great plains of the southern Ukraine and then up through Vinnitsa and Berdichev to Kiev.

That was the target. It was in the Ukrainian capital that he was to contact the defector, a scientist, he had pledged to spirit out of the USSR.

A journey of some three hundred miles through hostile country lay before him. But it would be only after contact was made that the real difficulties would begin.

First of all because the defector would be missed.

At once.

Second of all because this was no ordinary defector,
seduced by the decadence of the West.

The scientist wanted to leave the Soviet Union because in his opinion socialist principles in that country
were not applied rigorously enough, because communism and the ideals of Karl Marx had become subser-
vient to Russian nationalism.

The scientist figured that the only true disciples of
Marx and Lenin rented mailboxes in Peking rather than
Moscow. The defection in fact was not to the West but
to the East.

The route chosen was through Albania, south of Romania, Bulgaria and Yugoslavia, because the comrades
in Albania are Maoist rather than Moscow-oriented.
They follow the Chinese line and the Kremlin hates their
guts.

Bolan was posing as the Albanian agent sent to get the
scientist out, to spirit him past the security guards and
the KGB, to evade the genuine Albanian's contacts and
make it back to the border again.

But before he crossed that frontier a second time, he
had to convince the defector that the West was a better
bet.

2

It had started two months before in a house in Paris. The residence squatted in a quietly fashionable cul-de-sac a few blocks east of the Bois de Boulogne. The dwelling surrounded a central courtyard and was inhabited by only two persons: a wealthy old woman and her faithful chauffeur/bodyguard.

In her mid-eighties, the Grand Duchess Marijana Sophia Rytova was one of the few exiles from Czarist Russia still alive in the French capital. And the most bitter in her hatred of the country's new masters. Many regarded her as an eccentric, but the eccentricity lay only in the depth and ferocity of this hatred.

For many years, the duchess's fortune had been available to finance anyone whose aims were directed against the Soviets and particularly their most sinister arm, the KGB.

She had helped the Executioner once before in a private battle against the world terrorist Hydra. Now she was asking him to help her.

The telegram had simply said, AID REQUIRED FOR ANTICOM COUP STOP PLEASE COME STOP. Bolan was eager to find out the score as he paid the taxi driver outside the house.

Through the narrow wrought-iron gateway he could see the chauffeur, Alexei Kirov, lathering the yellow and black Hispano-Suiza landaulet the duchess had owned since 1926.

He wrung out the chamois and draped it carefully

over the handle of a bucket as Bolan walked into the courtyard.

"Good to see you again, Mr. Bolan," Kirov said, extending his hand.

Bolan nodded and took the man's grip. The thought came to the Executioner again, as once before it had, when he appraised Kirov. Knife.

Kirov was a young man who seldom spoke, doglike in his devotion to the duchess. But his quiet demeanor belied the murderous skill with knife and gun if the occasion demanded it.

"I am to take you to the basement before the duchess receives you," Kirov explained.

Bolan shrugged. "Uh-huh." He followed the chauffeur to a flight of steps leading down to the area.

It was here below ground that the mansion displayed the duchess's "eccentricities" at their most serious. The basement, which ran beneath the courtyard as well as the building surrounding it, was as modernistic in its decor as the gloomy rooms above were part of another epoch. The whole of the rubber-tiled floor space was occupied by sophisticated electronic gadgetry.

During the German occupation of Paris in World War II the property, like many in the neighborhood, had been commandeered by the Nazi military. The Gestapo had stockpiled a huge cross-index listing known and suspected left-wing sympathizers all over Europe and the Near East. After the Liberation when the house had been returned to private ownership and then sold to the grand duchess, a cellarful of files and dossiers concerning what the Germans considered subversive activity was discovered.

For the duchess this was a treasure trove in her unceasing fight against what she always termed "the Bolshevik horde."

Some of the material she handed over to the French

authorities. Files on those who had been no more than anti-Hitler patriots she destroyed. The rest—listing party members and their Russian contacts—formed the basis of an anti-Communist information center: a vast collection of facts and figures on every facet of Soviet activity.

With special concentration on the KGB.

But soon the sheer volume of material became unwieldy. Kirov was an expert, but sometimes it took him hours to come up with the answer to a simple query. A computer with the relevant information on its data banks could do the same job in one-tenth of a second.

So the duchess bought an IBM 650.

This was fine for sifting the increasing flood of information pouring from the noblewoman's worldwide contact network. But when the bloodstained hand of the KGB reached out beyond its original mandate as a committee of state security and started to manipulate not only individuals but terrorist groups and even whole governments in an orchestrated attack on the stability of the West, it became evident that a more sophisticated system was necessary.

The duchess's wealth provided it. Installed throughout the basement now was an IBM 7090. Connected to its limitless data banks were special input terminals that enabled the computer to be used for automatized functions such as the war games played by teams of experts at the Pentagon. "Although of course," Kirov told Bolan, "we limit ourselves to a single model here."

"Model?"

"Software jargon for a particular game. It is not a game in strict sense of the term, with a winner and a loser. What we have here is an attempt to create an insight-prediction situation—something that aids us in the assessment of probabilities."

"What does it do?" Bolan asked, tapping his fingers on the gray steel of a console.

"It checks out KGB agents and helps us get a line on their activities."

"You mean it keeps tabs on them?"

"We use the computer, after every morsel of intel on these people has been fed into its memory, to try and find patterns that we can interpret, and perhaps use to block some of those activities."

"And the system works?"

"Up to a point, Mr. Bolan, very well. But beyond that point...." Kirov shook his head and sighed. "The machine cannot predict. Not in the way we would like."

"Alexei, as usual, is pessimistic."

Bolan swung around. The grand duchess herself was standing at the foot of the stairway. It struck Bolan that for the elderly aristocrat, time had stood still. She hadn't aged a minute since he had seen her.

"In fact the computer is amazing. Almost any specific question about the enemy it will answer at once, providing of course that it is correctly put. What it will not do, what we very much wished it to do, is predict accurately the enemy's *future* moves."

"Sure," Bolan said. "Computers can only handle stuff that can be expressed mathematically, right? But how can you put a numerical value on guts?"

"Exactly."

"And you can't expect a fighting man to improve the performance of a computer. So what am I doing here?"

The duchess's face relaxed into a smile. "You had better come upstairs and have some tea," she said.

Bolan knew he was on to a big deal as soon as they went into the salon. Normally any anti-Soviet activity was prefaced by reminiscences, childhood stories of the grand duchess's hapless cousins, the Romanov children. But today, sitting beside the great gilded samovar in the souvenir-stuffed room, the duchess stepped out to bat right away.

"I shall give it to you straight, Mr. Bolan," she said. "A Russian scientist has improved a computer in the way I want. Using a completely new technique, he has created a machine that can in effect make inspired guesses. It is an associative memory process that allows the machine to range a million times a second over an infinite number of apparently unrelated data and make connections that resemble the human process of deduction."

The duchess sipped her tea.

Bolan said nothing. The duchess drained her cup. Bolan said, "So?"

"I want that machine. I want it here in Paris, and I want it soon."

Bolan laughed. "You have to be joking, ma'am! The computer you have takes up almost the entire floor space of the basement. How can you expect one that's most likely twice that size to be smuggled out—"

"I assure you I am most serious. Besides, you surprise me," the duchess reproved. "The computer in Russia must be destroyed. It is the scientist who must be smuggled out. So that he can rebuild another one here."

"Suppose he does not want to be smuggled out?"

"The scientist wishes to defect," Marijana said.

"Now I get the picture." Bolan put down his cup and leaned forward. "You want me. . .?"

"I want him to be brought here, but there is a problem." The duchess explained that the Russian computer wizard figured he could serve the cause of communism better in China than in the Soviet sphere. "Your job is to persuade him to defect to the West. The methods of persuasion I shall leave to you," she said. "But you must approach him in the person of Kriplin, an Albanian contact man. He is not due to make his run for several weeks, so you will have time to familiarize yourself with the background and the terrain."

Bolan sat back in his chair. "How do you know all of this?" he asked.

The noblewoman smiled. "There are many thousands, perhaps millions, of my countrymen who would like nothing better than to rid themselves of the enemy." She spread her bejeweled fingers. "Is it then so surprising, my friend, that it should not prove too difficult to find allies among them—for one who knows both the country and its people?"

"I guess not," Bolan admitted.

The duchess's two brothers and her mother, distant relatives of the Romanovs, had been executed, he knew, by the Bolsheviks during the October Revolution of 1917. The grand duke had escaped with the young Marijana through the generosity of an itinerant Gypsy circus that had once wintered on his estate on the Baltic. Disguised as members of the troupe, they had fled the terror eastward through Siberia.

They carried a large number of the fabulous Romanov jewels. The gems, coated with opaque varnish, were sewn to their crude costumes as though they were the glass beads popular with such performers at that time. But the wealth and security this collection afforded them in exile did nothing to erase memories of rape by a whole company of border guards when they reached Vladivostok, of the murder of the duchess's father by NKVD agents in Berlin in the 1930s.

No wonder, Bolan reflected, that her hatred of the Soviet regime bordered on paranoia.

"And this genius scientist who thinks the Russians are not far enough to the left, what do we know about him?" Bolan asked.

"Very little," the duchess replied. "Seems to be something of a mystery man. Name of I.K. Korsun, believed to be Latvian or Estonian, but none of the Western scientists who frequent these international conferences have met him, and he's listed in none of the official journals. According to my sources, he works out of the University of Kiev—the authorities give him a free hand there.''

''Nothing on your own computer downstairs?''

She shook her head. ''The only published reference— it was no more than a throwaway paragraph in *New Scientist*—was the acronym, the code name for his machine. It is known as RIAMS. It stands for Random Input Associative Memory Selector.''

She stood up and advanced her cup toward the spigot on the samovar. ''You will go in and get him out for me?'' she pleaded.

Mack Bolan simply nodded.

Two days later he took over the entire fourth floor of the duchess's house and began studying computer print-outs and large-scale maps of the Carpathians, deciding on the best place to crash the frontier into the Ukraine.

A week after that, geographers hired by the duchess arrived with a sheaf of satellite photos and started work on a sand-table model that stretched clear through three of the mansion's huge reception rooms.

Installed behind a rampart of research material, Bolan was able to pack in twenty-two days of intensive study before word came from the duchess's Gypsy friends that the time was ripe to cut the wire on the Romanian side of the frontier.

He climbed into her Cessna executive jet at Le Bourget airfield the following night, and fixed the straps of his parachute harness as Kirov lifted the aircraft out of France and roared toward the East.

3

Bolan crouched on the damp earth behind a clump of evergreens and listened. The trucks carrying reinforcements up to the frontier had rumbled into silence. Now he could hear nothing but distant shouts from the guards and, high above him, a breeze sighing through the branches of the forest trees. He breathed in the piny odors of the night. On the far side of the bushes, thorny scrub masked the lip of the old quarry where Schelgatseff would be waiting.

Or *should* be waiting.

During Bolan's one-man war against the forces of evil, experience had taught him to take nothing for granted. Not even terrain formations memorized after weeks of study: sand-table models and photo blowups, however accurate, failed to show such details as exposed tree roots, a fallen sapling, undergrowth that had spread since a photo was printed. Three days' labor by a lumberjack could wreck the orientation of a clearing and leave an undercover traveler with no place to go.

Bolan's night vision was excellent, but he had already ripped the side of his blacksuit on some kind of briar and twisted an ankle when his left foot sank into a rabbit hole. Now he parted the evergreens cautiously and strained his eyes to pierce the dark: if the edge of the quarry was closer than he figured, an untimely fall could abort the mission in a single second.

Yeah, the mock-ups had been okay. A pool of darker blackness on the far side of the scrub indicated the gap where the land had been blasted away. Bolan worked his way around, then down the slope toward the track that passed the quarry mouth. He threaded a passage through the bushes, felt with his right foot and found the edge. According to the photos he should be no more than six feet from the floor. He jumped down.

It was more like ten feet. And the floor was strewed with fragments of rock. Bolan landed heavily, wrenched his left ankle again and pitched forward, bruising both forearms.

He rose upright and limped toward the far side of the quarry. The car should be one hundred yards away, hidden beneath overhanging branches against the rock face. Ahead and a little to his right, moonlight materializing suddenly in a space between the clouds struck a gleam of brightness from a polished surface.

The car was there.

Cautiously, Bolan approached it. He could make out the square, dim outline of a medium-size sedan. Softly, he whistled the tune that had been agreed on as a recognition signal.

There was no reply.

Bolan frowned as he felt a warning prickle. Maybe the Russian had been scared off by the lights of the convoy passing the quarry mouth. Bolan whistled again, a little louder this time.

Silence.

He stifled an exclamation. Something was wrong. The man was supposed to wait by the car to brief Bolan on the route to Kiev and the military controls he could expect, before handing over the clothes and papers the Executioner would need. Even if the convoy had scared the contact temporarily away from the telltale sedan, he should have returned once it passed to wait for Bolan.

Moving toward the front of the car, Bolan stumbled

over an obstruction. Something soft. Stooping, he reached down into the darkness.

This time the exclamation was loud and clear.

Schelgatseff was waiting all right. He would wait a long time, as long as Bolan or anyone else wanted.

The big guy's exploring hand had homed on a gap where the back of the Russian's head had been. He drew it back, heavy with congealed blood and bone splinters. The body was still warm. At this altitude, in this temperature, that had to mean that Schelgatseff's skull had been shattered within the past half hour.

For the second time that night, Bolan cursed. He must risk a light—first to make a mental comparison with a photo of Schelgatseff that he had seen, then to see if the killers had overlooked any of the material he so desperately needed.

But the Executioner had no light. There was only one answer: the parking lights of the car. That should give him enough illumination without attracting the attention of the soldiers on the ridge above.

He put his hand on the door, feeling for the handle. The surface crumbled and flaked away beneath his fingers.

The car body was warm too.

One of Bolan's senses that had been clamoring for attention elbowed the other four aside. The night smelled no longer piny but acrid and bitter; the stench of burning caught his nostrils.

The sedan had recently been set on fire. The light he had seen from the far side of the quarry had been reflected from a single shard of glass that still hung in the scorched window frame.

If there had been any doubts in Bolan's mind as to whether or not he was blown, this dispelled them.

Rapidly he checked out the charred interior, searched the dead man's pockets and found nothing.

Something else was certain. The killers, whoever they were, did not want him to get far. He was alone in Russia with nothing but his bruised hands, a twisted ankle and a torn blacksuit to help him make the three hundred miles to his target.

With that chilling realization, a vital question surfaced. Was he up against the KGB, the Russian frontier forces or maybe even the CIA? Since the Stony Man debacle and the murder frame that followed it, when a price had been set on Bolan's head by the world intelligence fraternity, it could have been any of them.

The Executioner had always been a loner. But now, with the few Stony Man survivors he could trust forty-five hundred miles away, he felt more isolated than he had ever been in his life.

In the darkness, the muscles around his mouth tightened in determination. Okay, so he was on his own. And he would carry the thing through single-handedly. Long odds had never stopped Mack Bolan yet. He would go in fighting and do his damnedest to bring that scientist back alive!

Just one thing bothered him still. Bolan liked to know the odds. And there was a link missing here, a wild card that he could not account for.

If they knew enough to open fire while he was crossing the frontier, to waste his contact, destroy his cover and burn the getaway car, why hadn't they stuck around, waiting to jump him when he showed?

The question was answered sooner than he expected.

A spotlight beam lanced the blackness from the woods above him, flooding the quarry with brilliance. At the same time, automatic fire erupted all around the edge.

Momentarily blinded by the dazzling light, Bolan barely had time to hurl himself beneath the gutted automobile before a hail of lead smacked into the coachwork and rocked the body on its blackened springs.

4

Bolan's reflexes were supertuned. The involuntary life-saver that had flung him beneath the automobile as the guns around the quarry belched flame, fed urgent messages to his brain as he fell.

The messages encapsulated a single word: survival.

Before he hit the ground Bolan's mind was made up. Beneath the hulk of the sedan, he might be safe from shots fired by gunmen on the lip of the quarry above. But an unarmed man would be a sitting duck once they surrounded the wreck at ground level. Bolan's instincts told him he had to keep moving. Get out before they get wise.

He kept on slithering under the car. He was on his feet on the far side, between it and the rock face, before the guns fired their second volley. Creepers trailed down from the lip, and no marksman was posted directly above. The sedan itself would have restricted his field of fire.

Bolan seized fistfuls of the clinging growth and swarmed up the quarry face. He hauled himself over the lip as the guns—he guessed they were Czech-designed Skorpion machine pistols—spit fire once more. The spotlight was still focused on the rock-strewn quarry floor, where the body of Schelgatseff lay sprawled beyond the blistered fender of the sedan.

Ricochets and rock chips hummed through the darkness as the weapons blasted the wreck for the third time. Then gunners began deploying down the slope toward the quarry mouth, leaving three men firing short bursts on automatic to cover them.

Bolan rose from the night behind the nearest gunner as the man slammed a fresh clip into his magazine.

The guy was lying prone in the undergrowth, a dim silhouette in the reflected illumination from the spotlight. Bolan stamped his right boot on the ambusher's neck, then stooped and crooked a steely arm beneath the gunman's jaw, jerking back his head before he could cry out.

The guy threshed among the leaves, striving to escape the paralyzing grip. He struggled frenziedly to roll over and bring up the machine pistol. Bolan kicked the weapon away and planted a knee in the small of his back, increasing the pressure until the sweat stood out on his own brow and at last the man's spine snapped.

Bolan allowed the lifeless body to slump and felt for the machine pistol in the undergrowth. There was a cartridge belt hip- and shoulder-slung on the corpse, and he discovered to his astonishment as he unsnapped the clasp and dragged it away that the guy was kitted out as a civilian. Bolan frowned as he stared down into the quarry. Was the whole deal nonmilitary?

The gunmen were circling the burned-out sedan now, dim shadows outside the pool of radiance cast by the spotlight. Someone shouted an order and the beam, maneuvered from the lip on the far side of the quarry, shifted to encompass the rock face behind the wreck. The guns emptied once more, and a leaden fusillade hammered down between the wheels, striking showers of sparks from the stone floor.

One of the men stepped for an instant into the arena of brilliance. Hell, Bolan thought, the guys down there were also in plain clothes.

So whom had he come up against here? A counter-intel team? The KGB? Friends of the Albanian, Kriplin?

And what connections if any did these goons have with the border guards who had been waiting for him to show up above?

Bolan came up empty. Besides, there was no time for quiz games now. Space was what he needed...as much space as possible between this killer force, whoever they were, and himself.

Down below the killsquad was closing in. The Executioner left them to it and stole away between the trees. For two hundred yards reflected light from the spot aided him. After that the going became tough. But he knew there was a second trail angling up into the forest a quarter of a mile away, a rough track that split off lower down the valley from the route used by the military. He headed in that direction, traversing the slope, feeling every foot of the way lest the swish of a branch or a rustle of leaves betray him.

In the darkness behind, Bolan heard the voices fade and then swell to a crescendo. He knew the ambushers had discovered that their prey had already slipped the net. They would fan out around the quarry next—perhaps even search the far side of the trail—and then there would be a second outcry when the body of the man Bolan had killed was found.

The fact that he was now armed would make them advance more cautiously. A resolute man in dense woodland could wreak havoc with a patrol, especially at night.

Especially if he was a jungle fighter blooded in Vietnam.

And if the hunters knew anything about him—and so far they seemed to know a lot—then they'd know they were dealing with no ordinary soldier.

By the time faint shafts of light from the about-faced spot splashed the tightly packed trunks of the trees, Bolan was long gone.

Half an hour later he reached the second trail—dimly discernible as a swath of paler darkness that was matched by a strip of starlight gashing the black bulk of interlaced branches above.

Bolan stopped and listened. There were no sounds of pursuit. They wouldn't know which way to start. And it was unlikely, however serious the leak had been, that they would expect him to be so familiar with the lay of the land.

Bolan rested his back against a tree and took five once he had made the trail. His twisted ankle was throbbing and he knew from the tightness of his boot that it must have swollen badly. He unclipped the frames he had used when he crossed the plowed strip, and used the remainder of the rest period touch-checking the machine pistol he had won.

He knew at once he had guessed wrong. The weapon was not a Skorpion. The open wire stock that folded forward over barrel and muzzle was a different shape, and the gun was more solidly made and much better balanced.

But the general layout was similar—a stubby, two-handed weapon with short-recoil blowback operation, a curved 20-round magazine in front of the trigger guard and a rear pistol grip. Bolan guessed it was a development of the Skorpion known as the vz.75.

He had never handled the gun before, but he knew it fired a heavier slug with a higher muzzle velocity than the Skorpion's 7.65mm shot. From the feel of the rounds slotted into the cartridge belt he guessed the magazine was fed with 9mm Makarov ammunition.

He was hefting the machine pistol experimentally when the sudden sound of voices froze him against the tree trunk.

Two of them, male, Russian speaking, quite near— less than one hundred yards away, he judged. He could not make out the words but the rhythm and intonation sounded conversational, not the kind of exchange sentries would make at the end of a beat.

Who in hell could they be? Hunters? Trappers? Six thousand feet above sea level, at dead of night, half a mile from the Soviet frontier?

Bolan crouched near the ground and listened. Fifty yards downhill the pale blur of the trail vanished around a bend. The voices came from beyond the curve. A scrape of feet too. He rose upright and crept toward them.

From behind a pine sapling he peered around the corner.

A clearing. A wider expanse of sky separated the treetops. Two guys, no more than shadows against the trail, were standing smoking. And the red tips of their cigarettes reflected in a curve of polished metal.

Bolan made out the dim outlines of two big limousines.

The Executioner held his breath. Unwittingly he had backtracked on the route the murder squad had taken to the quarry. He supposed they had used this secondary track and then footed it through the woods to make sure there was nothing to tip him off around the rendezvous. The two guys he could see must be the drivers, waiting to transport the ambush troops back with their prisoners. Or with his corpse.

And the corpse of Schelgatseff.

How much did they know? Bolan mentally ticked off the events as they had unfolded so far.

They had known he was coming, they had known when and where, they had known about the rendezvous with Schelgatseff—and presumably, therefore, the cover he had intended to use after the meeting.

But did they know where he was going?

Probably not, Bolan reasoned, because if they did, it

would surely have been simpler to wait in Kiev until he showed and then nail him there.

Uh-huh. So the entire operation was not blown. But although this implied that they did not know the aim of his mission, Bolan's immediate problems were now one hundred percent more critical than if he had made contact with Schelgatseff.

He had no clothes, he had no cover, he had no vehicle.

And the nearest railhead was a single-track spur that ran from Beregomet to the junction at Glybokaya, on a secondary route linking Bucharest with Kiev.

Beregomet was forty torturous mountain miles away.

There was no other way to get there. Without a map, a compass and food, any cross-country attempt would be suicidal.

Bolan grinned in the dark. He'd cracked tougher ones than this in his one-man war against the wicked.

What the hell—he had a choice of two cars right here!

Padding softly along the edge of the trail, he approached the two drivers. One of them was talking in a desultory way about this nighttime foray in the cold when he could have been home snuggled up in a warm bed with his wife.

Too bad, comrade, Bolan thought to himself, but it's many a lonely night your wife is going to spend from now on. The Executioner snicked the machine pistol's selector to auto.

The positive, metallic click was not loud, but it was a dead giveaway in the forest silence.

"Who is it?" one of the Russians shouted. "Stay where you are. One move and you're dead."

The man who was speaking leaped for the nearer limousine, jerked open the door and snapped on the headlamps.

Bolan dropped to the ground.

The reaction had been quicker than he expected. In the tunnel of brilliance carved from the dark by the powerful beams, the man who had shouted caught the tail end of the movement. He was carrying a pistol, a heavy Stetchkin automatic. He fired instinctively, a single detonation that blatted back and forth between the tree trunks and sent awakened birds flapping angrily away from the upper branches.

Bolan scowled as he felt the wind of the slug above his head as it parted the long grass where he lay. Okay, the guy was a pro. He wasn't going to waste half a magazine until he could see the target.

Bolan realized he had to act fast. On full auto the vz.75 fires at a rate of 840 shots per minute. The entire magazine can be discharged in less than two seconds if the finger remains on the trigger.

Pinned down by the lights, with no chance to reload, Bolan could not afford to let the Russians separate. He must zap them both with a single burst.

Averting his eyes from the glare, he aimed the machine pistol just wide of the car door. The man who had switched on the headlamps had forgotten that the vehicle's dome light would also stay on, silhouetting them as long as the door was open. He moved frantically to close it, a Stetchkin already in his other hand.

Bolan squeezed the trigger.

The machine pistol belched flame, roaring and bucking in his grip as he hosed lead in the classic figure eight.

The ejected shell cases pumped out, glinting gold in the headlamp beams.

The Russian who had been trying to close the door took only two slugs. They hit him as a loop of the first eight was closing and the shots had begun to climb. Only two hits, but each drilled a hole above an eye and dropped him neatly.

The second man had begun a move toward his companion and was cut virtually in two by Bolan's death hail. The pistol fell and his body folded backward and disappeared.

A piece of glass detached itself from a smashed window and tinkled to the ground.

Bolan pushed himself to his feet and hobbled through a haze of cordite toward the car. That ankle was giving him hell now: he would have to find a mountain stream and fashion a cold compress if he was to remain active when daylight came.

Right now there were other things to do.

The killers at the quarry would come racing back once they heard the shots. Since they had no further need for concealment they could make it, he figured, in fifteen minutes.

They weren't going to find Bolan.

No slugs had touched the second car. The first had suffered a flat, a shattered windshield and doors that looked like slabs of Emmentaler cheese.

Bolan decided not to waste ammunition putting the vehicle one hundred percent out of commission. He unscrewed valve caps and deflated two more tires. Then he smashed all the lamps, wrenched off the distributor cap and stamped it into fragments.

Limping toward the undamaged car, he paused.

Radio?

Sure. Beneath the dashboard. A CB-type setup with handset. He pulled out fistfuls of wire and smashed the mike and receiver.

One minute later he was behind the wheel of the intact vehicle, gunning the engine as he raced downhill.

He had one hour before the moon rose.

5

As the limousine snaked perilously around the down-hill curves, Bolan reflected on the lifetimes, the seemingly endless road he had traveled—from his war against the Mafia to his head-on clash with the KGB and all the events that had occurred in between. To him only the names were different, the intent was essentially the same—the subjugation of decent individuals, indeed, whole societies.

And Bolan took it personally. He was a single warrior dedicated to the eradication of evil, in all its manifestations, throughout the world. His was an unceasing vigil in this war everlasting.

Bolan would fight eternally to hack off the Hydra heads of world terrorism.

The fight had already cost him dearly. Rejection by his own country, a price on his head outside it, the loss of his family, of the woman he loved. But he would go on fighting until he faced the supreme test, whenever it might come, or die in the attempt, and with luck the warrior image he had created in men's minds might carry on the battle even after that.

For that was the way Mack Bolan was fashioned. That was why he had accepted this present challenge, so different from many of his hit-'n'-git exploits, because its success—and the use of the electronic wizardry this would presage—would carry the fight one step farther into the enemy's camp.

And it *would* be a success, he told himself grimly. It

had to be. No matter how high the odds were stacked against him.

A disastrous start, okay, but already he was mobile. Next in line was the attention to his ankle. No sweat. After that he had to find appropriate clothing. And once again Bolan must call on his skill as a master at role camouflage. Because only after he was satisfied that he could pass, at least visually, for a local could he attack the problem of papers.

Bloodstains and bullet holes had ruled out the idea of an exchange with the drivers he had killed. He would have to find alternatives well before daylight.

But he could not afford to keep the car that long. The moon, rising in less than an hour, could bring helicopters. They could be overhead sooner if they were equipped with infrared night sights or searchlights.

He reckoned it would take the killsquad perhaps half an hour to hotfoot it back to the frontier once they discovered the two corpses and the wrecked automobile. On the rutted dirt road, iron-hard with frost, he wasn't going to make much more than fifteen or twenty miles in that time.

Less if the ambushers and the frontier guards were part of the same operation. If they were, they would be in radio contact. In which case the pursuit, army trucks from the border, choppers called up from the nearest military airfield, could already have started.

But were the two groups connected?

Bolan reckoned not. The car was a Zil—a limo developed from the postwar Packard Clipper that was normally reserved for Party big wheels or security officials. The Stetchkin automatics carried by the drivers had been withdrawn, Bolan knew, from Red Army service. Neither was the vz.75 army issue. He would lay his money on the notion, however crazy it seemed, that he had run up against two separate and unrelated attempts to block him.

In that case the chances were that the civilians were KGB. And because of the bitter rivalry between the two services, it might mean that the army officers at the frontier would argue before they cooperated.

Whatever, he had to get rid of the Zil soon.

And for the first time that night, luck ran his way.

First, somebody stole the car.

Then it began to snow.

Bolan had driven maybe ten miles when the first flakes fell. Storm clouds piled up and extinguished the stars, erasing the hint of brightness paling the eastern horizon as though a curtain had been pulled across the sky. Soon the white flurries streaming toward him in the headlamp beams in turn blotted out the road. He dipped the beams and reduced speed. Then he cut the beams, switched to fog lamps and slowed still more.

When five miles per hour became dangerous and the snow was building up on the windshield, he coasted to a halt. He opened the glove compartment. The wiper blades were inside. In Russia where auto spares were virtually nonexistent, Bolan knew, to leave the blades exposed was to lose them the instant your back was turned. He opened the door and climbed out into the blizzard.

Once the blades were in place, he looked around. The limo had rolled to rest at a humpbacked bridge where the truck crossed a stream. Fifty yards off the road were clustered half a dozen wooden shacks, slanted roofs already white against the somber forest trees.

Bolan limped across to the nearest cabin. He could smell farmyard odors, a hint of wood smoke. The folks inside would be opening their shutters and stirring soon.

He stole in beneath the overhanging eaves of a barn and stumbled onto a woodpile, grazing his shin. Bolan swore under his breath as he bent to rub the bruised spot. As he straightened up something whipped at his face and seemed to tangle around his neck. Taken off guard, The

Executioner swiped at the "attacker," his senses going into combat mode. Then, in relief his pent-up breath escaped as he realized what it was—two rough cotton shirts and a pair of canvas pants hanging from a line.

The garments were stiff but not yet frozen solid. He took them all and recrossed the roadway. Since he had stopped the car anyway, he might as well attend to his ankle now.

At the bottom of the bank below the bridge he tore one of the shirts into strips and plunged his swollen ankle into the stream. The icy water numbed the lower half of his leg as effectively as a judo blow.

He had soaked the improvised bandage and was winding it around the swelling when he heard the motor of the Zil burst into life. He heard the wheels fighting for purchase on a carpet of snow that was already freezing, and then the big car snaked away.

Bolan listened as the exhaust note faded. He shrugged. Good luck to the thief. He could not have wished for a better timed decoy. Whoever had taken the limo would have some explaining to do when he found himself surrounded by armed and angry helicopter crews and members of the KGB!

Bolan completed the compress and worked over the remaining shirt and pants with his hands until they were relatively pliable. Then he put them on over his blacksuit. For the moment he kept the machine pistol and the ammunition belt slung over his shoulder.

Back on the bridge, he started walking painfully downhill, the boot unlaced over the compress, the woolen mask protecting his face from the stinging assault of the snow.

Outside an isolated shack some way behind the hamlet, he found an ancient bicycle.

In some ways, so long as the route continued on down, this would be a better bet than the car. In a snowstorm it would be just as quick—maybe quicker if the wind blew any harder—and now that the thief could be relied on to draw off the pursuit, it would probably take him farther.

He wheeled the machine out onto the roadway, his boots creaking on the freshly fallen snow, and pedaled away. It was only then, when the rusty chain squealed in protest, that the dogs began to bark.

Bolan coasted on down, ducking his head against the snow squalls.

Once he thought he heard the distant clatter of helicopter rotors somewhere above the blizzard, but with the wind moaning through the trees on either side it was impossible to be sure. Later, he pulled off the road and lay prone to allow a small convoy—a scout car and a Red Army half-track full of soldiers—to slither past with motors roaring. An urgent voice jabbered from the scout car's radio.

Half an hour before dawn, Bolan reached an intersection at the foot of a valley. A wider, smoother road curved away to the left in the direction of Seletin. The route to Beregomet and the railroad lay straight ahead: a steep grade arrowing up through the pines on the far side of the valley.

Bolan abandoned the bicycle. Even if he had had the power in his wrenched ankle to force the machine up the slope, the surface was now frozen solid; the wheels would never have gripped.

He limped a short distance and then gave it up. He found a lumberjacks' shelter, a rudimentary log cabin, eighty yards off the road. He would wait there until daylight and then take a chance on hitching a ride into town.

Within ten minutes the fast-falling snow had covered his tracks.

6

Trucks collecting peasants for work on the cooperatives started to climb the hill soon after dawn. The moment he saw the first vehicle, Bolan gave up the idea of hitching a ride. The men and women packed swaying in the open body were swathed in furs, in layers of threadbare cloth, in sacking tied with string. They wore caps with earflaps or fur hats. None of them were hatless or clad in nothing but a shirt and pants. Not on this kind of day.

It had stopped snowing but it was penetratingly cold. Even with his specially designed thermal inners, Bolan was chilled to the marrow. Unless he wore the woolen helmet, the air he breathed seared the membranes of his nose and throat. It would be courting disaster in a country district, where every stranger was suspect anyway, to appear in public without more protective cover.

To avoid too much curiosity in the area, Bolan had boned up on an accent and certain dialect expressions that were typically Georgian. But even a stranger from more than eleven hundred miles away would not be so dumb as to chance the beginning of a Moldavian winter without some kind of topcoat.

Bolan knew that before he dared continue, he had to remedy that situation.

The opportunity did not arrive until nine-thirty.

A tractor pulling a four-wheeled cart loaded with sugar beets chugged down the road from Seletin and started to labor up the hill.

Bolan stepped out from behind a snow-covered juniper, the machine pistol in his hands.

The tractor slewed sideways when the driver braked, then slid to a halt with two wheels on the soft shoulder. He stared, half standing above the iron seat, a plume of breath twinning the exhaust fumes jetting from the tractor's vertical muffler. "What the devil—" he began.

"Into the woods, comrade. Inside the hut," Bolan ordered. "We have things to discuss." He motioned with the stubby barrel of the MP toward the woods.

"What do you mean? Who do you think—"

"Move!" Bolan's voice was a whiplash. The driver, a tall, truculent man, exchanged glances with a small black hole that was the eye of death. He swallowed.

Bolan said nothing more.

The driver climbed shakily down, leaving the tractor's diesel motor idling.

At the entrance of the hut he turned again. "I do not understand, comrade.. , .."

"You don't need to," Bolan snapped. Shifting his grip on the MP, he sword-handed the Russian between collar and cap flap, a stiff-finger blow that dropped the driver.

Bolan dragged him inside and stripped off the cap, a rabbit-skin wraparound with a rope belt and a pair of shaggy fur boots.

Bolan had no quarrel with the ordinary Russian people. He left his own boots and the woolen helmet beside the unconscious man. The guy would be unconscious for several hours, but at least he would not freeze to death under the log roof now.

With the gun and cartridge belt hidden beneath sugar beets, Bolan clambered to the tractor's driving seat and continued up the steep grade. Muffled up as he now was, with the cap flaps buttoned beneath his chin, he was practically indistinguishable from the original driver.

It was not an easy ride. He still had twelve miles to cover before he reached the railhead. And even the huge ribbed tires on the tractor's rear wheels found it hard to grip the icy surface. On the downgrades, tractor and trailer tended to jackknife and Bolan had to wrestle the wheel to prevent the combination broadsiding.

There was very little traffic. Bolan saw pickups loaded with lumber, hay, root crops. And an occasional bus and abandoned automobiles thatched with snow. At the foot of one slope, half a dozen men with shovels were digging a slat-sided flatbed crammed with squealing pigs out of a drift.

Nearer Beregomet, snowplows were at work, and the sanded road showed black between grimed banks of frozen slush.

Bolan had to make a decision. A guy driving a tractor was no problem; he could be going anyplace. But a trailer loaded with sugar beets was something else. It had to be heading for some kind of refinery. He had already drawn curious glances in one village, not joining a line-up of beet trucks waiting for the gates of a factory to open. In Beregomet he could easily foul up, arousing suspicion if he took the wrong direction.

But if he junked the trailer, he'd have to leave behind the gun and the ammunition belt with it. No way could he conceal them up on the exposed seat of a tractor.

Bolan took the risk. In town, a hick hauling a load could be told to go this way and that by cops, militiamen, an overseer, whoever. And shooting them down with 9mm slugs would not improve his chances too much.

Okay, he'd make it unarmed. He could always jump some guy for a gun later. On a deserted stretch of road, he backed up the trailer beneath the trees, threw gun and belt into a drift. He drove on into town, whistling, the flesh of his face raw from the cold.

He parked the tractor in back of the freight yard, where there were tankers, trucks and container trailers already littering the muddied ice between the tracks.

Beregomet was a small town, with snow on the roofs and not enough folks to turn the streets and sidewalks gray.

Not for the first time Bolan was struck with the drabness of Soviet life. It stemmed above all, he figured, from lack of choice—at every level from politics to breakfast. Oh, sure, there *was* a choice. You wanted to buy a watch, for instance, you had a choice of two. You could buy the man's watch or you could buy the woman's watch. If watches had been delivered to the stores that month.

You wanted to have stuff transported, you could decide between the panel truck, the pickup or the flatbed. But they all looked the same on the outside. Socialist delivery vehicles carried no slogans, no lettering: those gray panels could hide television sets, boots, cabbages, a consignment of beef.

Or a militia detail on special duty.

The doors burst open and a dozen men jumped to the ground as Bolan emerged from the yard. They were wearing long slate-colored greatcoats and flat army caps with shiny peaks. Each man carried a Makarov submachine gun, a holstered revolver and a portable transceiver clipped to his belt.

"A tall man, at least six feet," a noncommissioned officer was saying as Bolan drew near. "Weight around two hundred pounds. And most important of all, he walks with a pronounced limp."

Bolan froze in midstride. *How the hell had they known that?*

He had only been limping since he jumped into the quarry. Nobody saw him leave it and the guy whose gun he had taken was dead. So were the two limo drivers.

Somebody must have seen the tracks leading to the log cabin, slapped the tractor driver awake and raised the alarm.

The militiamen had not seen him yet. He steeled himself to continue on past the truck.

"Probably wearing a flapped cap with fur boots and a fox-fur coat," the NCO was saying as Bolan drew level.

The Executioner stifled a smile. Even in the home of "equality" the comrades looked after number one. The tractor driver was pretending his coat was a better quality than it was, unwittingly doing Bolan a favor.

Half a minute later and Bolan would surely have been asked to show his papers. As it was, the noncom was busy detailing his men, telling them which corners to patrol, as Bolan passed.

Beneath the cap flaps, Bolan gritted his teeth and forced himself to stride upright and even, through the piled snow, across the street and onto the opposite sidewalk. By the time he made it, his forehead, despite the cold, was beaded with sweat.

There were a few kopecks in the pocket of his stolen coat. He went into a *pivnoyzal*, a workingmen's beer parlor, and joined the throng of drinkers around the communal table.

"Stranger in town, comrade?" asked a burly, bearded laborer standing next to him.

"Passing through," Bolan growled. "On my way home to Tbilisi. I'm glad the winter hasn't started yet in Georgia. I must have been crazy, qualifying as a reforestation analyst when I could have studied marine biology and stayed by the Black Sea."

"You choose a good time to leave here," the bearded man said, "quite apart from the foul weather. Two escaped prisoners stole a KGB car last night, killed fifty soldiers and then tried to crash the frontier."

"There are rotten apples in every barrel." Bolan used the Russians' favorite noncommittal reply.

"Yes, comrade, but this is our barrel," the man said sourly. "And since they haven't caught them yet, you won't be able to walk a hundred meters in this town without some ape in uniform demanding your entire life history." He jerked his thumb at the steamed windows.

Two militiamen were examining papers on the frozen sidewalk outside.

There was a urinal in back of the parlor. The area beyond it was choked with trash cans and empty beer crates. Bolan glanced swiftly behind him, then climbed onto a pile of containers and pulled himself over the wall at the end of the compound.

He dropped into a beaten earth alley, grimacing from the jarring pain in his twisted ankle. The alley fed a street and crossed the main drag. Bolan hoped it led down to the railroad station. That was where he had to go. But first he was in this crazy situation where he had to put the hook on some guy, hold him up for money before he could even buy a ticket. With that and the ID checks, the sooner he quit Beregomet the better.

From the side street he saw that there were control points on either side of the intersection.

He had to make the far side unseen. After that he'd play it by ear.

A single glance right and left told him that there were no pedestrians on his side of the narrow alley. A cattle truck, a couple of private cars and a decrepit bus, momentarily held up by one of the militiamen, were waiting to cross the intersection.

Behind the fogged windows of the bus, passengers stared ahead, trying to guess the reason for yet another delay.

Bolan dropped to the sidewalk, rolled over the snow piled along the curb and slid beneath the bus.

The underside of the chassis was caked with frozen mud. Dirty gray icicles, formed from spray thrown up by the wheels, festooned the rear axle and cross members. Lying on his back, Bolan wormed his way head-first toward the front of the vehicle.

Just behind the huge gearbox, a subframe strut warmed by the heat of the motor offered an oily but ice-free hold. He reached up and wrapped his hands around it.

The bus jerked into motion.

Bolan flexed his arms, raising his shoulders and torso from the ground, allowing his heels to drag along the roadway.

The racket of the engine was deafening. Warm oil dripped onto one side of his face. Two inches from his ear, the open drive shaft spun greasily.

He was dragged painfully this way for perhaps 150 yards, and then with a hiss of air brakes the bus jolted to a stop.

They were in the center of the intersection. Boots tramped close to the side of the bus, halted near the doors, mounted the step. Bolan heard the scrape of feet above his head, louder than the throb of the motor.

Militiamen were running an ID check on the passengers.

He bent his head, squinting down the length of his body. It would be better if he could get his feet off the ground. Even if they didn't look underneath, the heels could leave tracks once the bus started again. And beyond a certain distance, friction would wear away the fur boots and pulverize the flesh of his heels.

Bolan guessed the station was about three hundred yards. Maybe a little more: it had been some way beyond the spot where he had parked the tractor. He reasoned the bus had to stop at the station. That's why they were checking out the passengers. To kill any chance of an escape by train.

And that was exactly what Bolan planned to do.

Bolan looked down the bus's underside again. The nearest cross member to his feet was the rear axle casing. He stretched the toes of his good foot. They were six inches short of the casing, which slanted down on either side of the differential housing. The only way he could rest his feet there would be to keep hold of the crossbar with his arms extended. And while it was hellishly difficult to keep his body off the ground with his elbows bent the way they were now, only a superman could do it at full stretch.

Bolan had to be that superman.

He gripped the strut hard and pushed, shoving his shoulders down toward the rear of the bus. At last he was able to raise one leg and rest the heel on the tubular axle casing.

Before he could lift the other, the militiamen climbed down and stamped away; gear selectors thumped into place behind Bolan's head and the drive shaft began to rotate again as the driver engaged the clutch. The bus shuddered forward once more.

Bolan's heel slipped and his foot dropped from the casing. He swore, straining arm muscles to keep his shoulders off the roadway as the bus accelerated across the intersection. Kicking upward, he found the axle casing again and lodged his foot there.

The driver shifted into second. The vehicle lurched and bounced over the frozen ruts, entering the station approach road.

Bolan was about to try for the other side of the axle with his damaged foot when he realized that if he positioned himself that way his body would be beneath the spine of the bus. And the shaft, spinning at several thousand rpm, could burn into his hip. Also the bolts of the universal joint, whirling dangerously near his head, could slice into him like a circular saw.

Tensing his leg muscles, he felt for a second foothold on the same side of the chassis, found a brake rod, felt it bend under his weight and finally crossed the free foot over his own ankle.

It was not a comfortable journey. His fingers, biceps, calves and belly muscles were on fire with the strain. Fumes from a leaking muffler choked his nose and mouth; oil dripped onto his eyelid and ran down into one ear.

Then icy water drenched him with the force of a blow, sluicing his back and shoulders as pebbles thrown up by the front wheels hammered the back of his head. The bus plowed through a hollow awash with melted slush and stopped outside the station.

Passengers clambered down, stamping the snow from their feet as they tramped into the entrance hall. Bolan was about to roll out from under and rise to his feet on the far side when there was a slither of tires and a second bus pulled up immediately behind the first.

He gritted his teeth. Impossible to let go now: the driver of the second bus would see him. He had to hang in there until the next stop. It was in fact no more than five hundred yards, but it seemed to him like a hundred miles.

The bus slackened speed but did not stop. One man jumped off and continued walking in the direction the bus was traveling. Bolan had seen from underneath that the near side of the road was bounded by a wall. He took a chance, allowed himself to drop on his back and rose upright as though pulled by a string as the rear of the vehicle passed over his head.

He looked around quickly. The bus stop was on a curve. The street was deserted with warehouses and offices on the far side. A sawmill beyond the wall. The passenger who had jumped off was crossing over to one of the buildings.

Bolan slipped through the gates of the sawmill. He was certain that no one had seen him. But if anyone did they were sure going to take a second look. He was covered from head to foot with freezing mud, and his hands and face were black with oil.

Some kind of overseer in leather boots and a fur hat was standing by a timekeeper's hut just inside the gates. He stared at Bolan in astonishment.

Bolan tackled the problem head-on.

"Goddamn bus drivers!" he raged. "Half the road is flooded and they drive through at forty miles per hour. Never give a thought to the people on foot. Have you any place here, comrade, where I could wash some of this grime off me?"

"Just a pump," the man said. "You'll freeze to death, comrade, but use it if you want. On the far side of that stack of lumber." He jerked his thumb toward an open-sided shed.

Bolan thanked him and walked painfully over, steeling himself not to limp.

The water was so cold that it scalded like fire. He cleaned up as best he could and surveyed the rest of the yard. The clothes he was wearing were now a little less scarifying, but unless he could get rid of them in the next few minutes they would freeze solid.

Behind the mill with its screaming saws was a freight shed. A forklift truck was loading lengths of planking onto the last of four flatbed cars at the rear of a train waiting to leave the timber yard and rejoin the main line.

There was a caboose behind the flatbeds. Half a dozen boxcars separated them from a steam-shunting locomotive hissing quietly by open gates at the exit from the yard.

Bolan permitted himself a crooked smile. Okay, here was the way out. If there was a brakeman riding the caboose, he wouldn't know it but he was due for replacement. If not, then either the caboose or one of the boxcars was going to harbor a non-fare-paying passenger as far as Glybokaya.

The money problem could wait. Right now, priority number one was to get the hell out of Beregomet. He walked around the corner of the freight shed and stopped three feet away from two young militiamen armed with submachine guns.

The taller of the two swung his nightstick and held out his free hand. He could not have been more than twenty years old but his face was as hard as granite. "Your papers," he said curtly.

Bolan plunged a hand between the stiffening lapels of his wet coat. "Of course," he said, a man suddenly remembering. "In the timekeeper's office. We do not carry them while we work."

Bolan was a head taller than either of the militiamen and a great deal more muscular, but there was something unnerving about the total absence of expression on those Slavic faces.

The Executioner was only too aware that, yes, he was in Soviet Russia, the fortress state whose iron grip extended over two continents, that these youths represented the most ruthless tyranny the modern world had known. Given the command they would shoot down women, torture children, launch a nuclear missile as heedlessly as a lumberjack swinging at one of the forest trees being sawed up at this mill.

And he was an intruder in their territory. He was an enemy of the state and the proof of his guilt lay in the fact that his pockets were empty.

"The hut," he said. "By the gates. I left them there with the overseer. As you see, I am wet. I did not wish to have them soaked as I worked at the gully."

"The other laborers here carry their papers," the shorter man observed.

"They are not working to clear a blocked drain," Bolan said. "And they are not casual workers, folk passing through like me. People are suspicious of strangers here. Keeping their papers ensures their good behavior."

"Perhaps they are right to be suspicious," the taller man said. "You will accompany us to the gates. And the papers had better be there."

"They will," said Bolan. He turned toward the gates and the two Russians fell in at either side and slightly behind him.

Bolan exploded into action. The militiamen were carrying submachine guns. In a single flow of movement he seized the barrel of the nearest, pushing it toward the ground as he jerked up the butt with manic force. He spun the weapon, breaking the man's grip on magazine and trigger before his finger could tighten, slamming him beneath the chin with the steel butt plate. At the same time he whirled ferociously toward the second man, bringing the two face-to-face in front of him.

The conscripts, who hadn't even known enough to keep their guns out of reach of a suspect, were so bewildered that Bolan was able to release the SMG and smash their heads together with stunning effect before they could react.

As they staggered apart he unleashed a murderous blow to the throat of one with the edge of his left hand, and then swung a great looping punch to the other man's jaw with his right. The blow, fueled by Bolan's frustration at finding himself unarmed with no money and no cover, carried all his weight. And all his anger.

The militiaman joined his companion on the ground.

Ten minutes later as the train pulled away from the freight shed, a tall militiaman wearing a greatcoat slightly shorter than usual swung aboard the caboose, his SMG slung over one shoulder.

"Orders are to stay with you as far as Storozhinets," he told the brakeman. "It seems they suspect those escaped prisoners may jump aboard."

"I thought you people always worked in pairs," the brakeman said dubiously.

"We do," Bolan told him. "My comrade's up front with the engineer."

Storozhinets, the only sizable town between Beregomet and the junction, was about forty minutes' ride away. Bolan reckoned that the bound, gagged and unconscious militiamen he had left beneath the platform of the freight shed would be discovered before they were halfway there. He figured the authorities would radio or telegraph ahead and have the train stopped some place along the line.

He was counting on that.

And he guessed right. They were crossing a wide snow-covered valley between steep slants of frosted pines when brakes squealed and the train shuddered to a halt with a clatter of buffers.

Bolan looked out of the observation window. The line ran along an embankment here, and there were army trucks drawn up between drifts on a country road below. At the front of the train, an officer was leading a detail of twelve men up the slope toward the locomotive.

"Now what?" the brakeman grumbled.

"Now this," Bolan told him. The right cross that connected with the brakeman's jaw did not travel far, but it traveled fast and hard and it was scientifically placed. The guy swayed for a moment on rubber legs and then sank to the floor.

Bolan's mind raced. The Russians had to believe that he had left the train and taken to the woods, preferably with a companion, as soon as he saw the soldiers. Only that way could he be sure that the heat was off. And only then could he take time off to attend to the necessities of life. Like money and papers and proper clothes.

The search party were opening the second boxcar when two figures appeared from behind the caboose and plunged down the embankment on the far side from the road.

The one carrying the gun was wearing no greatcoat, and the other, the guy with the greatcoat and cap, seemed to be in a bad state. His accomplice was supporting him all the way down.

The two men disappeared into a thick stand of trees that linked the embankment with the woods on that side of the track. There was a single burst of automatic fire from beneath the trees. The soldiers climbed, slid or leaped down the slope, firing as they went, and fanned out toward the trees.

Bolan lay panting in a culvert that ran beneath the embankment. They would soon find the unconscious brakeman in his borrowed robes. But since the grove of trees was thick enough to prevent snow falling between them, there would be no tracks. And the pursuers would naturally assume that the second fugitive had run farther into the woods away from the train.

This was Bolan's second premise. The third was that the last place they would look for a man who had escaped from a train would be back on the train itself.

And that was exactly where Bolan was headed.

The plan worked. The soldiers were drawn away. When their voices had faded in the muffled atmosphere of the snowbound countryside, he emerged from the culvert and scrambled back up the cindery slope of the embankment. Again, no tracks.

He was clutching the brakeman's jacket and fur hat. Later he would change the jacket with the militia tunic he was still wearing. For the moment he was content to lift the corner of a tarp on one of the flatbeds and crawl in among the resin-smelling stacks of lumber.

After a while the train began to roll again.

From time to time he peered out from beneath the tarp. The sky darkened, became sulfurous. He saw villages with beaten earth streets, painted wood churches with onion domes, cattle huddled beneath tin-roofed shelters in the snowfields.

Bolan hoped the authorities would assume that it was the two refugees who had stolen the limousine, had disposed of the brakeman and jettisoned his body somewhere along the line. Even when they discovered that the unconscious "fugitive" *was* the brakeman, nothing he could tell them would make them think Bolan had returned to the train. If they did capture the genuine escaped prisoners, any search for Bolan would remain concentrated on the area between Beregomet and Storozhinets.

Before the train reached the outskirts of Glybokaya, snow began falling again. Through the whirling flakes Bolan saw a refinery, gasoline storage tanks, the serrated roofs of a factory.

He breathed a sigh of relief. At last he was free of everything that had hit the fan when he was blown at the frontier. He had finally shaken off the pursuit.

There was only one flaw in his thinking. Rattling over the switches that linked the tangle of tracks forming the junction outside Glybokaya, the freight train curved right instead of left as he had hoped.

They were steaming back south into Romania.

7

A wintry shroud blanketed Kiev. The baroque pinnacles of St. Sophia Cathedral were already frosted with snow. On the fourth floor of a yellow sandstone building on the Malinovsky Prospekt, Major General Greb Strakhov sat frowning behind a huge desk, bare except for two telephones and a single sheet of paper.

There were twenty-two lines of Cyrillic typescript on the paper, and every single line etched the frown more deeply into Strakhov's brow.

Strakhov sighed. Without consulting him, the GRU—the military intelligence division of the Red Army general staff—had acted on their own.

And they had fouled up. The information on the sheet of paper in front of him was totally negative.

One of the telephones on the desk was a direct line to the KGB headquarters at No. 2, Dzerzhinsky Square, Moscow. The other—it was ringing now—was connected to a switchboard behind the building's heavily guarded entrance four floors below.

Strakhov picked up the handset. "Comrade General?" the operator's voice inquired deferentially. "The comrade Colonel Antonin of the Third Chief Directorate is waiting in reception."

"Have him brought to my office," Strakhov said curtly.

Antonin's directorate was responsible for KGB border forces and for the secret surveillance of the MVD and the armed services. The personnel were not popular with the military.

Antonin himself acted as liaison between the KGB and the GRU. Waiting for him to arrive, Strakhov stared at the single-sheet report for the tenth time.

He shook his head and slapped at the paper with the back of his hand. It had all started so simply, not even as an operation but as a banal counterintelligence routine. One of the KGB's Paris residents, running a standard check on some eccentric Czarist refugee, had discovered that she had installed a computer that was used for reactionary-deviationist activity.

Communications experts from the Thirteenth Regional Department, aided by technicians from Strakhov's division, had managed to arrange a partial tap.

But lacking the special key codes and operator identifiers permitting access to its data banks, all they could glean from the tap was a copy of the CRT printouts.

They could eavesdrop on the computer's answers, but they did not know the questions.

The CRT intel tipped them off that an illegal crossing of the Soviet frontier was planned in a mountainous area of the ancient province of Bukovina. The information specified times and dates. It even identified a traitor, an army captain who had been bribed to allow the intruder free passage across the border. Later programs fingered the man Schelgatseff and the cover he had been asked to provide for the mysterious agent.

But it did not identify the agent himself. And there was no indication of where he was going or what his mission was.

That would not have presented an insuperable problem if the GRU had not alerted the border guards, ordered the elimination of the agent, then allowed him to get away.

As a result, panicked by the shooting, Strakhov's own men had killed Schelgatseff before finding out all he knew. And then they too, unforgivably, had permitted the infiltrator to escape.

The Red Army captain, now in solitary at the Lubyanka prison, claimed to know nothing of the identity of the man he was to have let through. Strakhov was inclined to believe him. A few more days—perhaps hours—of "sharpened interrogation" would show whether or not he was telling the truth.

In the meantime an unidentified foreign spy, possibly a saboteur, was at large somewhere in the Soviet Socialist Republic of Moldavia. And so far he had eluded all attempts to trap him.

There was a discreet knock on the door. "Come," Strakhov called.

Colonel Antonin was a thickset man with a shaved skull. He came to attention before the desk, clicked his heels and ducked his head. "The comrade general wished to see me?"

"Ah! Dmitri Aleksandrevitch!" Strakhov said genially, as if the visit was a total surprise. "What have you got to say for yourself?"

The colonel swallowed. Like the rest of Strakhov's subordinates, he was scared of the man. Anytime Strakhov used the familiar patronymic form of address, it meant trouble was on the way for sure. He studied Strakhov covertly as he considered his reply.

To a career soldier like himself, Strakhov was something of an enigma.

He was ruthless, formidably intelligent, calculating. Yet physically he was unremarkable—a gray man, middle-aged, of medium height and mousy coloring. Only the eyes, deep-set and burning, betrayed the ferocity of Strakhov's inner force.

At the moment, however, Colonel Antonin was concerned less with Strakhov's physical characteristics than with a question of geography.

Why had the comrade major general traveled all the way from Moscow to Kiev to take personal charge of what was, after all, no more than a routine police matter?

He cleared his throat. "It is regretted, comrade General," he said stiffly, "that there is nothing to add to the overnight reports from Moldavia. The...fugitive...is still at liberty. It seems clear now that the two escaped convicts were only coincidentally connected with the man. They made off with an official car that he had already stolen."

"They have of course been caught?"

"Ah...not as yet, comrade General. But the car has been found abandoned near Lvov, not far from the Czech border."

"Thank you, Dmitri Aleksandrevitch, I am familiar with the location of Lvov."

"Yes, sir. Of course," Antonin said wretchedly. "I hope—"

"They are to be shot the instant they are in the hands of the police. I do not wish our own personnel to waste time on them. It would seem that quite enough of that has been wasted already."

"Very well, comrade General. It appears that there is in fact only one foreign spy at large. It is my opinion that the clumsy attempt at the frontier to give the impression that someone was leaving the country rather than entering was nothing more than a tactic to gain time."

"Indeed? Time in which, had it not been for the idiocy of the GRU, we would ourselves have laid hands on the man at the quarry? Since you are strong on deduction today, Dmitri Aleksandrevitch—and since also you are our contact with them—how would you explain their decision to act unilaterally at the frontier?"

"Their officials are low in the Party hierarchy," Antonin said. "They feel themselves treated as second-class citizens. The capture of this man—if the coup had succeeded—would have been of great prestige value to them."

"If it had succeeded. It did not. Neither did our own. Even so, how do you account for the fact that this interloper—a man we know to be without transport or proper clothes or a cover identity—how do you account for the fact that he is still, it would seem, free to come and go as he pleases?"

Antonin was saved from answering by a knock on the door. A thin blond woman in a uniform skirt, a white shirt and a necktie carried in a small tray on which there was a glass of tea in a stainless-steel cradle and half a dozen slices of lemon arranged around a saucer.

Strakhov nodded and the woman went away. He picked up a wedge of the tart fruit, bit into it, blew across the steam rising from the glass and sipped the tea.

"We must remember, sir," Antonin said, "that the GRU knew nothing of our own plan to trap this man."

"Must we?"

Antonin coughed and tried another tack. "If the comrade general considers the matter of sufficient importance to bring him all the way from Moscow..." he began daringly.

Strakhov did not answer. The colonel was straying dangerously near a point that he, Strakhov, was reluctant to concede.

The point was that, although Kiev was his birthplace and he was always glad of an excuse to return, his true reason for taking charge of the operation was strictly personal.

The Paris resident had reported continual visits to the house near the Bois de Boulogne by the one man Strakhov hated most in the world, the one enemy against whom his implacable anti-Western hostility was directed at man-to-man level.

Mack Bolan.

Bolan who had killed Strakhov's only son, Kyril, a military test pilot, in a previous impertinent raid on Soviet territory. Bolan who had several times already thwarted carefully laid plans of Strakhov's in several of the world's hot spots. Bolan whose antiterrorist crusade was the single factor most likely to diminish the KGB's credibility and thus discredit Strakhov himself.

Was it possible that the foreigner who had so insolently evaded the Soviet security forces here and now was this same Mack Bolan?

Strakhov hoped with all his heart that it was. The chance to lay his hands on the man they call The Executioner was too precious to be missed.

He drained his tea glass, picked up another lemon slice and bit into it with evident relish. "No effort is to be spared," he told the colonel, "to catch this man. You may draw upon the reserves of all the security services. The entire resources of the state are at your disposal."

He stood up and walked over to face Antonin. "But in any event he is to be brought before me, dead or alive."

8

The deathbringer chattering in The Executioner's steely grip plastered the two militiamen against the warehouse wall.

For an instant one remained crucified against the brickwork, then he slid slowly to the earth floor and flopped forward with outflung arms. The second man, spun around by the force of the leaden stream, was slammed across a packing case. His fur hat fell to the ground, soaked with the blood from a gap in the back of his skull.

Bolan stood for an instant with the smoking SMG in his hands. Blue cordite fumes rose lazily upward to haze the dust motes vibrating in a shaft of sunlight slanting down through a skylight high above. The echoes of gunfire died away. Bolan had perhaps thirty seconds before the initial shock subsided and the noise drew workers and soldiers in from the freight yard outside the warehouse.

He acted quickly. The first of the militiamen had been on permanent guard duty inside the warehouse; his fur hat and greatcoat hung on a hook by a glassed-in office section near the entrance. Bolan put them on. The body of the second man was less damaged. Bolan whisked a billfold and a leather ID folder from his breast pocket, kicked off his own bedraggled boots and removed the Russian's.

Carrying them in one hand Bolan raced for an iron ladder spidering upward and swarmed silently toward the French-truss girders supporting the roof.

The great shed was used for the storage of Romanian grain destined for the Ukraine.

Above huge hoppers that fed the railroad wagons strung out along the track running through the building, there was a catwalk. Bolan raced along it in socked feet, gun in one hand, boots in the other, as workers rolled aside the doors and streamed in to see what had happened.

At the far end of the catwalk a steel-grid observation platform overlooked a bucket chain that was loading the last of the hoppers. The whir of belts and pulleys, the hiss of falling grain and the clatter of the buckets, which trundled up through a hatchway from a Romanian freight train in the yard below, drowned any noise Bolan could make there. Hastily he pulled on the boots.

Through the opening he could see weak winter sunshine on a patch of snow crosshatched with railroad tracks. He found a door that led to an outside stairway and walked down to the yard.

It was less than a quarter of an hour since he left the train. It seemed longer. The freight yard had provided the first opportunity for him to jump off since the locomotive had turned south: one of the boxcars was shunted off into a siding there and he had been able to crawl off the flatbed in the shelter of a coal dump.

He had no idea what town he was in. Could it be Siret? No, that was on the Romanian side of the frontier. What the hell, there was a railroad: he would simply wait his opportunity and somehow make a train heading back north.

He had been on his way out of the yard when the militiamen spotted him. He took refuge in the grain store, but they cornered him and were about to shoot him down without even checking his ID, when Bolan flipped open his stolen brakeman's jacket and raised the SMG.

Whether he had got away with it depended on the

presence or absence of witnesses...and how well the townsfolk knew the militiamen stationed there.

Most of the workers in the yard had crowded into the warehouse to join the rubberneckers around the dead soldiers. Bolan slung the SMG over one shoulder, pulled the hat low down over his forehead and walked purposefully out through the gate. In the distance he could hear the wail of a police siren.

It wasn't really a town: one long street following the curve of the railroad, a line of two-story, slate-tiled clapboard buildings, a gaunt brick cooperative headquarters. And behind, the inevitable slopes of snow-covered pines.

Bolan guessed it was a settlement that had grown up around a marshaling yard for frontier traffic.

Small, shabby cars—Trabants, Wartburgs, a Syrena—stood half buried in drifts that had been swept from the sidewalk. By the time Bolan approached the station half a mile away, the sunshine had vanished and dark storm clouds covered the sky once more.

The scream of the siren swelled in volume. A buff and red militia car skated into view around a curve beyond the station and broadsided to a halt in a shower of ice a few feet from Bolan. The car—the Russian equivalent of a patrol wagon, for the militia is the police sector of the MVD—was a Volga. A major in uniform rolled down the rear window and leaned out.

"You!" he called to Bolan. "What's going on here?"

Bolan snapped to attention. "Smugglers from across the border, comrade Major. Two of our men shot in the freight yard."

"My God, first they ask us to look for spies, now it's smugglers!" the officer complained to a man in civilian clothes who was sitting beside him. "Why don't the KGB do their own dirty work?"

Bolan watched as the civilian leaned forward. He was presumably of senior rank, an investigator perhaps.

"Why are you walking away from the scene of the disturbance?" he asked Bolan.

"A doctor," Bolan said calmly. "One of the men may survive. But the telephone line is down. It's just beyond the station."

"Then get a move on, man," the major snapped. "In these cases every minute may count."

Damn right, Bolan thought grimly as he hurried away along the slippery sidewalk. It could be half an hour before someone got wise to the supernumerary militiaman and the fact that no doctor lived beyond the station; it could be five minutes. His getaway depended on the local train timetable.

There were perhaps fifty people waiting at the station, most of them huddled in sheepskin, coney or musquash. There was a train too, but the doors were still locked. Evidently this was the terminal for locals not crossing the frontier.

Wind whistled around the cast-iron pillars supporting the canopy. As Bolan flashed the red militia ID he had stolen and passed through the gate, snowflakes too whirled down, settling on the packed ice that veneered the platform.

Bolan strolled to the front of the train. From the shelter of a plate-layers' hut, he called up to the engineer, who was leaning out the side of his cab chewing at a stump of sausage. "How long before you roll, comrade?"

"As soon as she goes green, comrade," the engineer replied, jerking his thumb at the signal lights. "Could be a minute, could be an hour."

"I have orders to travel with you as far as Chernovtsy," Bolan said. "It seems there are hoodlums around who may try to jump the train."

"You'd have a job going any farther," the engineer said. "That's where we stop." He finished his sausage and spit into the snow. "Come up here in the cab, you'll find it warmer."

Bolan emerged from behind the hut, glanced along the platform and scrambled up onto the foot plate. None of the passengers stamping the cold from their limbs appeared to have noticed.

The locomotive was a small saddle tanker with no separate tender. Bolan felt a blast of heat as the fireman swung open the smoke box door and shoveled coal. A bell tinkled in the cab. The engineer pulled down a lever. There was a hiss of steam and the doors of the four-car local slid open. Two minutes later the platform was empty, the light changed to green and the train jerked forward.

CHERNOVTSY WAS A SIZABLE TOWN with streetcars and lineups outside the food stores. The snow was falling heavily now, the soft flakes settling wherever they fell, muffling the sounds of footsteps and traffic. Bolan saw to his surprise that it was only noon.

It was no sweat quitting the station: he moved briskly among the countryfolk who had come to town for marketing. Perhaps there were a few more *boubas* in black shawls and headscarves, but otherwise, striding past the befurred men and women turning up their collars against the snow flurries, he could have been in any town in northern Europe.

Just the same, he thought, he had to get rid of the uniform and transform himself into a simple Russian, fast. By now radio, phone and telex receivers would be humming with descriptions of the phony militiaman who had shot down two blameless officers in the execution of their duty. Apart from which, police forces in Russia were no different from those anyplace else: a certain number of operatives patrolled a given area, all of whom would know each other, so a stranger wearing their uniform would automatically be suspect.

In a side street between an employment bureau and a market produce exchange, Bolan found a government clothing store.

There was enough money in the billfold he had taken from the dead militiaman to buy him a sweater, trousers and a checkered wool lumber jacket, leaving him with cash in hand. In the local equivalent of Moscow's GUM department store, he bought a cheap plastic holdall, stuffed the package inside and added underclothes and a rough cotton shirt.

His next problem, he figured, would be to find a place where he could change into the new stuff unobserved and, more importantly, dispose of the military rig. There was only one serious contender, the washroom at the railroad station; there should be enough coming and going there for nobody to notice that a guy who went in wasn't dressed the same way when he came out.

In the cubicle he stripped off the torn blacksuit and, not without a pang of regret, pulled the tab that started the self-destruct. He'd be gone before the phosphorus smoke was noticed. Quickly he pulled on the new clothes, keeping the regulation-issue boots—he could, after all, have been ex-military—and, after he had removed the red star, the fur hat.

Then he pushed the uniform and the brakeman's jacket through a transom into an empty cubicle next door and hurried away. He retained only the militia ID pass card and the few remaining rubles from the billfold, which he ripped apart and dropped into a litter bin.

Once the change was complete and he was clear of the station, he felt some of the tension drain out of him. The pattern of his behavior as far as the authorities knew of it should indicate that he was planning something in the frontier region. Maybe it was a good thing that the freight train had taken that southbound switch after all. In any case there was no good reason why anyone should start looking for him over two hundred miles away in Kiev.

For Bolan, once he got there, the life of an outlaw should ease up some. Gypsies and dissidents, friends of the grand duchess, were to contact him and advise on the best way to get next the electronics wizard, I.K. Korsun. Maybe they would be able to fix him up with a reliable cover too.

For the moment it was reward enough to feel secure in the knowledge that an ID check on the Kiev train was unlikely.

By three-fifteen, a ticket purchased with the rest of his stolen money, he was wedged into a wooden compartment along with a soldier, three peasant women toting cloth-wrapped bundles of vegetables and a group of laborers.

Sometime that evening, after one intermediate stop at Vinnitsa, Mack Bolan should have completed the first hazardous stage of his odyssey and should find himself at large in the Ukrainian capital.

9

Major General Strakhov plucked a slice of lemon from the bottom of his empty tea glass and chewed on it thoughtfully. He shuffled the papers that littered his desk and picked up a buff-colored sheet with the KGB Secret seal across the top left-hand corner. The information on the sheet, he read, had been abstracted from a classified CIA dossier photographed by a Soviet agent in the United States. The extract was headed: Mack Samuel Bolan.

Much of the material encapsulated in the report Strakhov already knew. He was familiar with Bolan's Army record, his fight against the Mafia, his more recent activity as head of the covert Stony Man operation. Strakhov himself had been the architect of the conspiracy that had disgraced Bolan and caused the death of his woman.

Strakhov's eyes homed in on two paragraphs that seemed particularly to interest him. The first revealed that at one time or another Bolan had been wanted for questioning in connection with more than two thousand homicides. Five federal police agencies, the state police of twenty-one states and almost a dozen foreign authorities had also classified Bolan as Wanted at various times during his career. Even the CIA had been added to the list.

With such a record—Strakhov picked up another lemon slice: the acid tang of the fruit seemed to sharpen his deductive processes—who could conceivably have wished Bolan to infiltrate the Soviet Union? And for what purpose?

If the intruder in southern Moldavia, who now had several more deaths marked up against him, was indeed Bolan.

Strakhov stared at the second paragraph. He read: "Mack Bolan was decorated with two Purple Hearts, a Bronze Star and a Silver Star during his military service."

As a very young officer, Strakhov himself had been decorated for distinguished service in the Finnish campaign of 1940, so he knew the extra edge required in battle action.

The major general permitted himself a wry smile, trying unsuccessfully to dismiss the grudging admiration he felt for Mark Bolan.

Strakhov rose to his feet and walked to the window, his hands clasped behind his back. Why would a man like Bolan break through the frontier defenses into Moldavia? The place was nothing but farm and forest; no secret installations were sited there; the nuclear warning system was no different from that in the neighboring Soviet states—less up-to-date if anything. Why Moldavia? Why?

He could think of only one reason: because the crossing would be easier there than anyplace else. It wasn't only the warning systems that were becoming outmoded in that part of the Carpathians. The fact that the man had succeeded proved the point.

It followed then that Moldavia was no more than a stepping-stone to some other region. Which? The Black Sea coast and the Odessa naval complex? The Baku oil center on the Caspian? A night landing from a small boat or a clandestine frontier break from Turkey would be easier in either case. Turkey again, or even Afghanistan, would be a safer bet if the new missile sites beyond the Urals were the target. But target for what? Sabotage? Spying?

Satellite photos could ferret out more details now than any individual agent, and as for sabotage...what would be the point? What could one man do? And what intelligence group in the West would employ a freelance like Bolan? In any case, according to the cover documents the man Schelgatseff was supposed to have delivered, no explosives were involved and the validity of the papers was strictly local: Bolan would never have got within a hundred miles of any of those areas.

The target then must be someplace in the Ukraine itself. In that case, why the devil had he turned south again toward Romania, once he was in?

To poison the grain supplies coming in from that country? The idea was preposterous.

Strakhov looked at the pieces of citrus fruit on the saucer and snorted. He was not coming up with any satisfactory answers. Maybe the lemon was not working today.

Still, he allowed the possibilities to simmer in his mind as he paced up and down, pausing every now and then to stare at a large map of the region that hung on one wall.

In the street below it was dusk, the sounds of traffic deadened as the snow fell more thickly. Lights pricked the darkness beyond the flakes illuminated in the glare from his window.

At six o'clock Strakhov rang for his secretary and asked for his hat and greatcoat. An agricultural trade fair, with union delegates invited from all over Europe, was due to open in Kiev, and he was obliged to attend the inaugural ceremony in one hour's time.

It was a puzzled man who left the yellow sandstone building a few minutes later.

A chauffeur in military uniform, saluting, held open

the rear door of a Chaika limousine. Strakhov nodded and climbed in.

Three minutes later he saw Mack Bolan.

Strakhov's mouth fell open. It was no more than a glimpse, a visual flash, one man wearing a checkered lumber jacket in a crowd surging out of the central station. A tall man with blue eyes, a square jaw and an intense hawklike expression beneath a Russian military-style fur hat.

But there was no possibility of an error. Not for a man whose image of that face had been forged in the fires of hatred for many months.

It was Bolan, no mistake.

Strakhov shouted to the driver. But it was the evening rush hour, the traffic was dense, the street slippery, the sidewalks crowded. The Chaika pulled a U-turn and slithered back the way it had come.

But the man in the lumber jacket had vanished.

10

At eight o'clock in the morning a guide from the Kiev Intourist office shepherded a group of twenty visitors into Kalinin Square. Bolan tagged on as unobtrusively as he could while the visiting trade-fair delegates followed the guide around and listened to her spiel.

The snow had stopped falling during the night. Except for a cloud bank low on the southern horizon the sky was a pale clear blue, but the wind blowing in from the plains beyond the Dnieper was bitterly cold, and the formal gardens in the center of the square were still humped with frozen white.

Bolan had slept fitfully in the back of a truck parked with hundreds of others behind the vast exhibition hall housing the trade fair. He had spent his last few kopecks on coffee and a hot sausage near the station. Now he was obliged to perform certain actions in a particular order, as a kind of visual code that would identify him to the grand duchess's contact, who would be on the lookout someplace in the great square at this time every day.

The geometric pattern of macadam walks separating the lawns and shrubberies had been swept clear of snow but apart from the Intourist party few people walked there. Beneath the leafless trees, workmen in caps and earmuffs stood around a row of small kiosks selling roasted chestnuts, newspapers and hot borscht.

Bolan was tense and alert. Next to a file of cream-colored single-deck buses, he saw drivers slapping their shoulders cross-armed, stamping the roadway in an attempt to keep warm as they awaited the dispatcher's order to move off.

The Executioner knew the contact would not be direct.

That would be too obvious. And too dangerous in a country where every second person could be an informer or a spy. But if the duchess's invisible messenger was satisfied that Bolan was Bolan, there would be a message waiting for him later at a drop point whose position he had committed to memory.

The party was approaching a ring of wooden seats that surrounded a frozen ornamental fountain.

Bolan drifted away from the delegates. He paused for a moment with one foot resting on the lip of the basin encircling the fountain.

Opening move.

A fringe of icicles spiked the plinth from which the water normally sprayed. Bolan walked across the ice to examine the snow-covered statue of a happy worker that surmounted the plinth.

Move number two.

Bolan turned, glanced at his watch and retraced his steps, walking back toward the buses along the whole length of the square, a tall solitary figure carrying a plastic holdall.

Alone in enemy territory, with no civilian ID and a submachine gun in that satchel, he felt more exposed, more vulnerable than at any time in his fighting career. He would have felt even more at risk had he known that his old adversary Strakhov was in Kiev, had indeed put out an all-points calling for Bolan dead or alive and organized a dragnet involving every available man on police duty in the city.

Maybe it was because he did not know, because the wide space of Kalinin Square was the last place a man in hiding would choose to be, that he got away with it.

He had noticed that there were more militiamen around than usual—groups of two or three controlling every intersection leading to the square. But he had paid them no mind. It was time to make the third move that would confirm his identity to the duchess's contact.

He approached the bus drivers and asked if there was a direct connection to the town of Lvov or would he be better off taking the train.

When he had been told that there were two direct bus services a day but that the first was not due for another hour, he turned to leave the square. The Intourist woman was on her way back with her flock in tow.

Bolan decided to visit the Church of St. Andrew.

Although it is a long way behind Moscow and Leningrad, Kiev, with nearly two million inhabitants, is Russia's third city. The old town, a trade center linking Byzantium with the Scandinavian empire a thousand years ago, is built on a plateau overlooking the curve of the Dnieper. At noon, Bolan leaned over a parapet and stared across the river at a sprawl of refineries, chemical factories and engineering works constructed since World War II on what had once been a swamp.

At 12:15 he descended a broad flight of stone steps to a promenade following the course of the Dnieper's right bank. There was a row of slatted seats at the outer edge of the paved walk. He turned right and sat on the third seat from the steps.

Below the promenade, traffic, lighter than it would have been in a Western city, skated along a riverside drive. On the dark water, gray ice floes swirled through the reflection of flames belching from a blast furnace, racing south toward Dnepropetrovsk, Odessa and the Black Sea. It was colder than ever.

According to Bolan's briefing, one of the slats forming the seat should be loose, leaving a gap between the wood and the cast-iron curve supporting it.

It was.

He crossed his legs. Setting the holdall on the seat, he looked casually around. Only one other bench was occupied: a Red Army soldier and his girlfriend, huddled together fifty yards away.

Bolan lowered his arm and moved the loose slat. If nothing had gone wrong, if he had satisfied the unseen contact or contacts watching the gardens in the square, there should be a message for him between the wood and the iron. This was the drop point.

His fingers curled around the end of the slat.

A thin scrap of paper, folded and refolded, wadded into a mass not much larger than a quarter. He eased it out between his index and middle finger, remained still for two minutes and then moved his hand to his knee.

The paper specified a rendezvous, a time and place where the duchess's friends would wise him up on the best way to contact I.K. Korsun.

Five minutes later, he looked once more at his watch, rose to his feet and sauntered down a farther flight of steps to the embankment.

Two hundred yards away, a bus picked up five people who had been waiting in a steel and glass shelter. While the shelter was still empty, he walked inside and unfolded the paper.

There was a single line of Roman script penciled on it.

St. Sophia. North transept. Chapel of St. Stanislas. 1355.

Bolan chewed up the paper and swallowed it. He walked briskly away from the shelter, looking for another flight of steps leading up into the old town. He found a curving stairway opposite a river bridge. He climbed slowly: he had eighty minutes to make the date.

Around the final curve three militiamen stood waiting with unholstered automatics in their hands.

Bolan did not pause. "Papers?" he asked wearily, feeling for the zipper of the holdall.

"Save them for the jail," the oldest of the militiamen growled. "With your height and that lumber jacket, that's all we need. Put up your hands."

One of Bolan's hands, as though searching for papers, was already plunged deep between the open edges of the bag's zipper.

He found the trigger and fired the SMG from inside the holdall, using the whole magazine, spewing death upward at the three Russians.

The muzzle blast shriveled the plastic and set fire to the synthetic silk lining of the bag. The militiamen dropped and the steps ran red. Only one had reacted quickly enough to shoot, and the slug had seared fur from the side of Bolan's hat and ricocheted off the stone wall retaining the stairway.

Bolan threw down the flaming container together with the now useless gun.

He snatched the pistol from the lifeless hand of the nearest militiaman, stuffed it in his pocket and then turned and ran.

Three times he was forced to double back among the narrow cobbled streets and alleys of the old town in order to avoid militia patrols. He arrived at the cathedral with only six minutes to spare.

He had no time to even think about it now, but he knew they were on to him. Right. That crack about the lumber jacket and his height proved that. Those were no routine patrols out there: he was in the middle of a manhunt and he was the quarry.

He knelt behind a wrought-iron screen in the dark side chapel and waited. A single candle burned among dusty artificial roses on the altar. Behind him in the huge dark vault of the nave, faint odors of mildew and damp cloth overlaid the smell of incense.

Moisture seeping in around the snow-covered dome above the bell tower ran down the pillars and pooled on the stone floor. Pigeons flapped in the chill gloom overhead. By the flickering light of the candle, Bolan could see the peeling remnants of a mural.

Whispered words echoed from the far side of the cathedral, and Bolan was unaware of the slither of feet until the bearded man in the black soutane was standing beside him and a deep voice murmured, "Into the box."

At one side of the chapel there was a fretted wood confessional. Bolan squatted by the kneeling spar on the penitent's side and waited for the priest to slide back the panel. Inside the octagonal structure the dank air reeked of decay and the wood was rotted and crumbling.

"You are fortunate to be here," the priest said after they had exchanged the verbal recognition codes agreed with the duchess. "There is a general alert out for you. Your name and description have been given to every militiaman in the city."

"My *name*?" Bolan was incredulous. "They are looking for me by name? I can understand that they might have traced someone, some foreigner here, but how could they possibly—"

"I do not know. I only know that you must do what you have to do very quickly and leave. Otherwise it will be dangerous for all of us."

"Can you fix me up with some sort of cover?"

"Something that will suffice at the university, yes. And papers that will be acceptable as long as you remain in Kiev or its environs. We can transform you into one of the delegates to the trade fair."

"But I thought you said I had to get the hell out?"

"That is so. I repeat, we can give you cover as a delegate and help you get to the university, but after that you will have to help yourself. There is not much time. We must hurry."

"What's the rush right now?"

"Occasionally, as a great favor—" the priest's voice was bitter "—we are permitted to move in a small procession from this place to the presbytery. On certain special days. This is one of them, and we must move on schedule or the permit is withdrawn."

"I don't get it—"

"The materials for your cover are at the presbytery," the priest explained. "And so, you see, you must come with us."

Ten minutes later, black soutanes plastered against them by the freezing wind, a small group of priests emerged from the door of the sacristy and followed the cross, the bell and the swinging censer through the twisting lanes of the old town.

Bolan was wearing a soutane too, hunched in the center of the procession to minimize his height, the headband of his black miter sliced away so that the crown rose no higher than the others.

The telltale lumber jacket and fur hat had been stuffed into a furnace that was supposed to heat steam pipes running beneath part of the cathedral. But he still carried the militiaman's pistol in the waistband of his pants.

The journey—it was no more than a quarter of a mile—passed without incident. Militia had cordoned off all the access roads bordering the route.

By the time darkness fell, Bolan was dressed in a cheap brown suit of synthetic fiber and a black leather overcoat in the style of the German SS. A woolen cap with earflaps and a visor was pulled low over his eyes. His boots had built-up soles and no heels, which cast his weight backward and forced him to adopt a splayfoot, shuffling gait that masked both his muscularity and his height.

According to the dog-eared papers he carried, he was Kurt Zimmermann from Leipzig, a shop-floor overseer in a factory that manufactured radio and television parts. The invitation and pass to the trade fair bore a more recent photo than the ID. The duchess was good at that kind of detail.

The fair's theme was trumpeted as Industry in Agriculture, and displays in the exhibition hall ranged from combine harvesters through crop-spraying equipment and cultivators to the enormous machines used in the Russian collectives.

Delegates were also permitted to view certain experimental projects and research exercises inaugurated by the university's mechanical engineering faculty.

It was adjacent to this department that the electronic laboratories housing the I.K. Korsun computer program were situated.

THE FOLLOWING MORNING Bolan walked up the broad flight of steps beneath the nineteenth-century Doric columns of the main university building together with twenty or thirty other foreigners.

Several hundred delegates had been invited to the fair, and until the first plenary session of the conference later in the week, they were free to circulate in the city or take one of the special tours organized to show off Ukrainian collectives or factories in other towns.

Militiamen were on duty outside the faculty building, but so long as the visitors wore trade fair lapel badges specifying their names and the factories they represented, they were allowed to roam wherever they wished.

Except for the experimental electronics department.

Some of the men and women who had entered with Bolan had been hived off at one laboratory or another, and there were no more than six left when he approached the far end of a quadrangle beyond which were the concrete buildings of the mechanical engineering faculty.

Bolan walked up to an archway labeled Electronics. A

militiaman stepped out from behind the stonework and barred his way. The man was carrying a Kalashnikov AKM automatic rifle. "Sorry, comrade. This section of the university is closed to the public," he said.

"I am not the public." Bolan showed his lapel badge.

"Delegates too. No entry here."

"But it is important for me to see." He fingered the badge once more. "I work in television and radio. The latest—"

"I said no." The Russian cop's voice was raised. He shifted his grip on the AKM. "Now beat it."

"They distinctly told me at reception—"

"Save it." The man was angry now. "I have my orders. You don't get in. Show me your papers."

Bolan fabricated the resigned sigh of those accustomed to bureaucratic officialdom. He moved closer, reached for his hip pocket. "Perhaps this will change your mind," he said quietly.

Bolan fisted the militia pistol. He was close enough to seize the barrel of the AKM with one steely hand and jam the muzzle of the automatic into the cop's belly with the other.

The Russian's jaw dropped. "Quiet, or you stay silent forever," Bolan threatened. He glanced rapidly left and right. The quadrangle was deserted. "Turn around," Bolan ordered.

Slowly the cop obeyed. Bolan reversed the gun. It was a new type Tokarev with which he was unfamiliar, but there were eight 9mm parabellum shells in the clip and the butt was heavy.

He struck viciously behind the cop's ear. The guy hit the ground like a sack of grain.

Bolan reckoned he could count on a couple of hours undisturbed, even if the cop was able to get released from the broom cupboard as soon as he recovered consciousness.

The Executioner walked down a long corridor, past closed doors with professors' names on them, past open doors showing workbenches littered with wiring. There was a hint of ozone in the sterile, conditioned air and everywhere around him a subdued, barely audible humming.

In a large room banked with gray steel control decks that blinked red, green and blue as pilot lights flicked on and off, he found three students: an African, a blond guy who could have been from any country in northern Europe and a girl who looked Vietnamese. They were working on a complex of transistors and printed circuits.

Bolan had removed the lapel badge. Here, he had to pass for someone connected with the faculty. His wrenched ankle was less swollen today, but the deliberately uncomfortable footwear still imposed on him a curious walk, half shuffle, half limp. He put all the authority he could into his voice.

"Professor I.K. Korsun?" he demanded haughtily.

The African looked up. "Dr. Korsun is at work on some very delicate—"

"I did not ask what he is doing," Bolan interrupted harshly. "I wish to know where he is."

The students looked at one another and then at him. "We have strict instructions—" the Vietnamese began.

"I, too, have strict instructions," Bolan snapped. "Strictly for you. The chancellor wishes to see Dr. Korsun at once. Unless you inform me instantly where he is to be found, you will find your names before the faculty disciplinary committee. Do I make myself clear?"

The blond frowned. "That is all very well, comrade...?"

"Commissar."

The student shrugged. "Comrade Commissar. Very well, if you insist." He jerked his head toward a glassed-in cubbyhole at the far end of the laboratory. "At your own responsibility. Through the overseer's office, along the passage and the third door on the left. It is downstairs in the sub-basement. But you must not enter unless the green light shows. The work is extremely—"

"I know about the work," Bolan repeated brusquely. He strode toward the office.

Students in a Russian university should be familiar enough with political interference, he figured, to dare no further action.

Two floors below ground the humming was louder, the dry air cooler. A green light glowed above a heavy steel door.

Bolan shoved up the weighty locking bar and walked into a small control room with padded soundproof walls. Through double glass he could see a long vault gleaming with switch gear and flashing lights.

A tall young woman wearing a white lab jacket was stooped over a two-chair console in front of a display screen, on which green lines of Cyrillic script ceaselessly scrolled.

As Bolan came into the room, she looked over her shoulder, angry at the intrusion.

He retained the same hectoring tone of voice. "I have to see Dr. Korsun. It is important. They told me—"

The voluptuous young woman rose upright and turned her back on the computer keyboard and printouts. "Who are you?" she demanded. "And what do you want with me?"

For one of the few times in his life, Mack Bolan was totally flustered. His eyes widened. No wonder the students above had looked at him so strangely.

The defecting electronics wizard he had come so far to hijack was a woman.

Bolan could see a tweed skirt and a blue silk top showing from beneath the white coverall. The woman's short pale hair framed a beautiful face. Clearly this woman, as the Russians said, "had access."

At over six feet and two hundred pounds, Bolan was a big guy. The professor was built to the same scale. She could not exactly look him straight in the eye, but she was unusually tall, big hipped, full breasted and radiating an animal vitality. Her mouth was wide and her eyes matched the blue of the shirt.

"Who are you?" she repeated angrily.

Bolan recovered from his astonishment enough to reply. "The name is Kriplin," he said. "I did not expect. . . . They just told me I.K. Korsun. . . ."

"Ingrid Karen," she told him. "I come from the Soviet republic of Estonia on the Baltic. We do not use the patronymic the way the Muscovites and Ukrainians and others do. Otherwise I would be I.B. for Ingrid Borisova. What are you doing here?"

"I thought we had a date," Bolan said.

"Not here. Not like this. Arrangements were made—"

"I had to change them," he interrupted. "I ran into some difficulties at the frontier." Bolan almost smiled at the understatement. And he knew the less they touched on any organization involving the real Kriplin, the better. The duchess had been able to tell him very little on this score, only that the man was personally unknown to the defector.

"I do not understand." Ingrid Korsun looked bewildered. "I was definitely told—"

"*I'm* telling you." There was fierceness in Bolan's voice. "We have to alter the whole routine. It is very important that we leave immediately."

"If it is really necessary. But why—"

"Questions later. Believe me," Bolan said truthfully, "it really is necessary."

She made up her mind. "Very well. You know I am under surveillance, of course?"

Bolan nodded. "KGB, I suppose. General or specialized?"

She smiled faintly. "Only general. So far. I am not yet suspected of deviationist tendencies or thought to be a revisionist. Rather it is I—in private, of course—who charge *them* with those crimes against the socialist ideal."

"Uh-huh."

"It is just that my work is valuable to the state, and so an automatic watch is kept on my movements lest in some way it should be lost to them...or wrested away. It is naturally—" the smile this time was scornful "—for my own protection."

"Naturally."

"It has been suggested," Bolan said, "that RIAMS computer could be used, against the interests of the true Marxist-Leninist society you wish to join."

Bolan cleared his throat and continued. "Also, we thought that the system here should be...placed out of reach...of the nationalist-revisionists and rebuilt to your own specifications in the East."

"Yes, yes," she said impatiently. "It was agreed that the machine should be destroyed and another built in Peking. Much of the paperwork has already been sent, and the rest I carry in my head."

"There is a problem." Bolan hesitated. "Because of

the frontier trouble I ran into, I don't have any suitable detonator or explosive.''

Ingrid Korsun laughed aloud. It was a pleasant change, Bolan thought, from the dialogue. She shook her head. ''It is not necessary.''

''But I thought. . . a small charge in a vital part that could wreck the whole system.''

''My poor friend, I tell you it is unnecessary. You must know there has been a lot of secrecy surrounding the development of this computer?''

''Yes, of course,'' Bolan said. ''And that's probably why so little is known about yourself.'' He grinned. ''Even your sex.''

''Precisely. No papers have been published, at least none detailing the specific theory involved. This was to prevent electronics experts in other countries exploiting my basic concept, which is totally new.'' She turned back to the keyboard. ''But it has left me extremely free insofar as the actual programming is concerned. And in fact it is perfectly possible for me and only me, to engineer a program under which the associative memory process will—how do you say—will eliminate itself.''

''You mean you can make it self-destruct?''

''Yes. Not physically but mentally, as it were. To use the computer I have to punch in my identification and my fail-safe codes. Others—not many but certain faculty members and high military officials—can do this. But only I have the secret of an overriding security routine that can negate everything effected by any other operator.

''The normal security system can be reversed. I can write a program that will erase all the material in this and associated computers' data banks. The program will automatically annul any subsequent orders to the contrary.''

''Can the program be written quickly?''

"Yes. In a matter of minutes."

"Do it," Bolan growled.

She settled herself at the keyboard, punched in her access and started tapping slowly...a few keys...a pause...a few more...a sudden rush and then a longer pause....

Bolan watched as she flicked the pages of a notebook covered with scrawled formulas of a kind he could not identify.

Along the far reaches of the vaulted room beyond the glass, he could see white-coated figures moving. At least one would be working for security. Maybe there was a second detailed to watch *him*. Bolan flattened himself against the wall as near the door as possible. Did the woman have enough outside visitors for an extra one not to arouse suspicion? Or were all of them automatically screened? If they were, that left him out on a limb: the mere fact of his appearance would be damning.

In any case, once the three students were wise to the fact that he did not even know their professor was a woman, surely they would have tipped someone off that there was a stranger in the house?

Whatever the answers, right now the last thing he must do was ask Ingrid Korsun herself. As Kriplin, he was supposed to know these things.

One thing was certain. The two of them had to get out of there.

Fast.

She had finished her work at the keyboard. She snapped shut the notebook and stood up.

"Is there any way out of here," Bolan asked, "without going back up to ground level and through the laboratory?"

"Yes," she said. "One floor up. The ordinary basement. There is a door and a flight of steps leading to Electrical Engineering."

"That's where we're going," Bolan told her.

She picked up a gray astrakhan coat and a matching hat. She put them on and opened the door.

They were halfway along the corridor that led to the stairway when they heard urgent footsteps. They froze. Behind them a man in a white laboratory coat was leading a group of four civilians on their way to the sub-basement. "It is probably no more than a coincidence," they heard him say, "but the comrade professor does not usually...."

Bolan was at the door in three strides. "Up," he ordered tersely, jerking it open and hustling her toward the stairs. "We don't have much time."

They emerged in a small courtyard bounded on three sides by workshops whose wide windows revealed benches of electromagnetic equipment. Ingrid pushed her way past glass doors into a hallway tiled with brightly colored mosaics. At the far end beyond another pair of doors, an ornate portico framed snow-covered campus lawns crosshatched with pathways.

"Where are the watchers?" Bolan asked as they hurried down the steps.

"The watchers?"

"You said you were under surveillance."

"I said general." Again she was impatient. "Nobody is detailed to shadow me all the time, if that is what you mean. Here at the university, my movements are noted. It is possible that an informer in my apartment house reports what visitors I have. If I were to leave by the main gates now, earlier than usual, it might be reported too. It is possible that a patrol car might be alerted to stop me and ask where I was going. But that is all."

"What about alternative exits? Would it be 'usual' for you to go over there?" Bolan nodded toward the far side of the campus where the arched roof of the exhibition palace rose above the conference hall attached to the university.

"Yes," she said. "I am due to lecture there at 1430."

"Fine," Bolan said. "That is where we'll go. You have a right to be there as a lecturer. And I—" he pinned the badge back on his lapel "—have a right to go in as a foreign delegate."

They had to cross a side street to reach the exhibition hall. At the far end a group of militiamen were checking papers at the university's main gates.

"That is *not* usual," the woman said. "Not at this time. They must have been warned by those men the lab assistant took down to my control room."

"We should split up," Bolan said. "If they catch up with you and you're alone, you can always say some crazy character busted in to see you, and after you got rid of him you figured you would make it to the lecture hall early in case he came back. If they really did put out an alarm already, that is."

"They will have done," she said. "In the case of anyone considered security sensitive it would be normal to try and locate them in this situation. If only to ask for an explanation."

"Right. Where do we meet inside?"

"By the Intourist desk. I have an idea how we might get clear of the city, but it depends on several things—particularly on whether we can make it before my lecture is due to start. Until then they will not know definitely that I am on the missing list."

Bolan nodded, turned and left her.

She crossed the roadway; he waited for two minutes. Red letters six feet high spelled out in Russian along one side of the building: When the World's Workers Unite Nobody Will Lag Behind! Spaced out beneath the huge slogan were six separate entrance doors. There were a number of private citizens mingling with the delegates entering or leaving. Bolan chose the door carrying the heaviest traffic.

The Intourist desk was beyond the main exhibits,

behind a dozen rows of photo displays, blueprints and diagrams detailing the various phases of the convention. Ingrid was already studying one of the charts.

Bolan edged up behind her and pretended to peer at another. It was safe enough to talk. Massive marble walls, topped with a lacework of iron girders that supported the arched glass roof, turned the exhibition hall into a sounding board that echoed as much as a nineteenth-century railroad station. Over the jabber of two thousand voices there was no risk from eavesdroppers.

As if considering a choice, Ingrid placed a finger against one of the notices pinned to the board. Bolan saw that she was indicating a conducted tour—one of the optional attractions offered to delegates. It took in a model collective farm and a show factory ten miles outside the city.

"I can't wait!" he murmured in her ear.

"What did you say?"

"You figure we should make the trip?"

She answered, still without looking around, "It will get us out."

"Won't there be checks? The cops? The KGB?"

"Not until after 1430, when I don't show for my lecture." She stabbed her finger at the notice. "This tour leaves at 1300, quite soon. If there are tickets still available, we must go."

"You mean there won't be any kind of check? Like those guys were making at the gates?"

"You come from the south, from the Mediterranean. You do not understand the Russian mind. It is bureaucratic. If the accounts balance, nothing can be wrong."

"I get it. But once they know for sure that they are short one professor of electronics, then they make with the heavy stuff all around, right?"

"That is correct. Let us go to the ticket desk."

"There's one other problem. The priests—that is, the

folks I was with last night—they were able to give me some money but they didn't have a lot. I don't know how much...."

She turned to stare at him. "I have money. Plenty of money," patting the pocket of her astrakhan coat. "Surely you remember? It was all agreed. I should finance any necessary expenses at this end and once we arrived in Tirana—"

"Sure, sure," he cut in hastily. "Of course. After all this frontier hassle and everything going wrong, I guess I forgot."

She looked at him again, frowning. And then, "Leave this to me," she said. "The tour buses depart from the main entrance. Wait for me there. I will join you in ten minutes." She walked away toward the Intourist desk.

There were tickets available.

Bolan stood on a curving flight of steps a hundred feet wide. The entrance to the palace had been built in the structuralist style beloved as "social realism," complete with an enormous bas-relief of jolly, smiling workers. He was staring up at the concrete-faced women with their sheaves of stone corn when the astrakhan coat brushed past him and a slip of pasteboard was thrust into his hand.

Admit one to Coach 33. Tour 15A, Bay 7. Departure time 1300 hours, and the date.

Coach 33 was a modernistic fifty-seat Volga with an observation deck and a large area of laminated glass. Bolan was five places behind Ingrid in the line waiting to board it.

The two hard-faced young militiamen scrutinizing tickets were armed with Stechkin pistols.

Bolan felt the familiar tingle of immediate danger at the nape of his neck as he approached. But the engine of the bus was already idling. Another was waiting to swing in behind it, ready to take a different group. The hands of the clock on the exhibition tower pointed to 1301.

The nearest militiaman glanced at Bolan's ticket and shoved him impatiently toward the door. "Come on, come on," the other man called to the delegates behind Bolan. "We are already late."

Bolan climbed into the Volga and took a seat at the rear, a few places behind Ingrid Korsun. From here, on the upper part of the deck, he could survey the whole length of the bus.

The seats filled with men and women, most of them indistinguishable from the Ukrainians on the street. A whistle blew. The hydraulically operated door hissed shut and the coach slid away across the hard-packed snow. Ten minutes later they were on the expressway that crossed the Dnieper and arrowed eastward across the white wastes of the plain.

Bolan was just beginning to relax when he looked toward the front of the vehicle.

Standing beside the single seat reserved for the Intourist guide with her microphone were the two militiamen, still carrying their Stechkins.

12

East of Kiev the snowfall had been lighter. From time to time, sheltered from the icy steppe wind by woods, black earth striped green with shoots of winter wheat broke the monotony of the bleak snowscape.

Bolan saw none of it. Throughout the journey he was desperately trying to impose some order on a mission that had become chaotic.

The important thing was that he had escaped the KGB trap, contacted his target and made it safely away from the watchers.

So the first half of the operation was wrapped up.

But that was the easy part.

Getting out again would be a problem. Blasting two fugitives through the frontier was more than twice as difficult as slipping one in. Also, Bolan realized, he soon had to confess that he was not an Albanian secret agent, that he had made the snatch under false pretenses. And, perhaps even more difficult, would be the task of persuading an idealistic, possibly fanatic Communist that the West was a better bet than the East.

That would have been tough enough without any other bad breaks. But the duchess's original plan had involved contact with certain dissident groups she knew who would aid them on the way out. That was now a no-go situation because it was Schelgatseff, and not the priests in Kiev, who had been the tip-off for them.

Add the fact that the electronics wizard turned out to be a woman.

From the few words they had exchanged, all Bolan knew about Ingrid Korsun was that she was a determined lady and that she had guts. She had to have if she was prepared to quit Russia and make for China on moral grounds.

How the hell was he going to convince such a character to stick with him, not just call the whole thing off and turn him over to the Soviets?

Bolan sighed. He could think of only one way.

He had come out ahead on tougher ones, but most of them had been where the action was. Playing it by ear was all very well during a night raid on enemy positions in a jungle. But when the jungle was urban, the enemy a network of civilians spiderwebbed through every social level, it was better to start out with some kind of blueprint for that action.

Because an organization like the KGB, operating a worldwide conspiracy of subversion, corruption and murder at second hand, could come up with some nasty surprises on its home ground.

The operative word was organization. A loner up against it could find himself in the position of a guy lost in a maze, not knowing which way to turn.

The Executioner grinned. They were playing his kind of game, in his court. *Direct* action was the answer.

Bust straight out.

Leave the dialectic until later.

On the outskirts of a small town, the coach turned in at the gates of a factory. Beyond serrated workshop roofs, squat chimneys stood sentinel over a row of ten-story workers' apartment blocks.

Bolan noticed a reception committee waiting by the office block.

Half of it was clearly composed of selected factory representatives: an overseer in a peaked cap; workers, male and female, in spotless white coveralls; a bulky man in a Khrushchev suit, standing a little apart, who looked as though he could be the director.

The other half were in uniform, cradling machine pistols. In front of the group, a noncommissioned officer holding a heavy-caliber automatic was speaking into a radio transceiver.

The coach door sighed open.

The noncom signaled to the cops inside the vehicle. One swung to the ground and hurried toward him. The other stood guard at the top of the three steps that swung outward when the door opened. The driver and the Intourist woman were watching with raised eyebrows.

The militiaman left the NCO and climbed back aboard. One of the other men advanced and stood below the steps. The two guards at the door motioned the delegates nearest the front of the coach to descend. As they filed out, the cop who had spoken to the NCO ordered each to produce his or her papers.

Bolan stood in the gangway behind Ingrid Korsun. "They must have discovered that I didn't make my lecture," she murmured, "and radioed ahead to check any bus, train or plane that left the city since I was last seen."

"You have ID?"

"Of course."

"In your own name?"

"Of course," she said impatiently. "You were to provide cover documents for the journey. That was agreed. Don't you have them?"

"Uh, no. That was one of the things that went wrong," Bolan said. "So this is a routine check? Until they see your papers. But once they're wise to your identity, that's it?"

"Yes. If they see them."

"We must make sure they don't." He was smiling.

This kind of situation was his specialty. Mentally he was flexing muscles, a boxer raring to leap out of his corner.

All the passengers in front of Ingrid had now left the bus. The Intourist guide got out. The militiamen beckoned impatiently. "Hurry, comrade. A routine check, but time is limited."

Ingrid pretended to be searching for something beneath the seat. Bolan stood aside to allow the delegates behind them to squeeze past.

Apart from a tall, thin, saturnine man wearing a fur-lined trench coat, they were the last two on the coach. Ingrid rose to her feet, buttoning her coat to the neck. The cops were waving them forward, scowling. "What do you suggest?" she said as Bolan edged past to take the lead.

"We'll take a ride on our own."

And then for the second time that afternoon, Bolan was astonished. "I'll handle the driver," she said calmly, "if you can look after the men with the guns."

He nodded, urging the man in the trench coat to pass ahead of them. But the thin guy halted in the gangway, an arm outstretched. "After you, comrade," he said politely.

Bolan shrugged. He would have to take his chance.

A militiaman's hand was already out, waiting for Bolan's ID. He produced the East German documents and then, as the guy took them, seized his wrist, jerking the Russian forcefully toward him. At the same time Bolan's other hand streaked out to grab the stock of the machine pistol, thrusting it upward.

Taken completely by surprise, the militiaman pitched forward into the gangway, tripping on the top step. His finger tightened on the trigger and the gun roared, spewing a hail of lead through the roof.

Bolan's knee jerked up. He twisted sideways, wrenching the cop around as a shield between himself and the second man.

But the second man was no longer there. He was on the floor by the Intourist woman's empty seat, fighting to regain possession of his gun. The thin man in the trench coat was astride his chest, one arm flailing and the blade of a knife glinting in his other hand.

Aiming to cut down an aggressor, the soldier on the ground outside the door fired a short upward burst, an angled shot that should have shredded Bolan's body from knee to waist. But Bolan had planted a foot on the first man's chest, shoving him violently outward as he snatched back his papers. The stream of 9mm slugs drilled the militiaman between the shoulder blades, spraying a curtain of blood on the glass of the door.

The driver was shouting. From the corner of his eye, Bolan registered Ingrid's gloved hand flash slantwise to the man's carotid. The driver keeled over his wheel.

Before the dead guard's riddled body hit the ground, the man outside fired again. But Bolan had dropped to the floor, the Tokarev pistol now in his hand. The heavy automatic bucked and jumped as the slugs sped out and smacked into the Russian's flesh.

The impact of the bullets, traveling less than ten feet, hurled the man backward onto the snow. A lacework of scarlet webbed out from beneath his back but froze solid before the pattern was complete.

Beyond him the NCO had been talking to the last delegate to leave the coach—a fat woman who had been sitting next to Ingrid. By the time he had pushed her out of the way and shouted to his men, the hydraulic door with its bloodied glass was shut.

Inside the coach, the thin man was on his feet. He no longer held the knife. The long blade had disappeared through the soft flesh beneath the militiaman's jaw, transfixing tongue and palate, penetrating the brain.

The haft projected below his chin. Twin trickles of blood rolled from the outer corners of his eyes.

Ingrid had dragged the unconscious driver from his seat. Now Bolan took his place.

The 250hp Volga motor was still idling. Bolan slammed the lever into Drive and trod on the gas pedal.

He swung the wheel hard over as the NCO's automatic spit fire and the machine pistols of his men chattered their litany of hate.

Fat studded tires scrabbled on the slippery surface of the yard, spouting a fan of slush over the shooting soldiers. Glass all along one side of the coach shattered. Slugs starred the windshield. And then the bus was screeching around in a tight circle, the heavy rear end dancing left and right on the slippery ice as Bolan steered for the open gates.

Ingrid rose from the gangway where she had been sheltering. The tall thin man was now coolly sitting in the Intourist woman's seat. None of them had been touched.

Bolan braked, slid the coach left onto the roadway and gunned the motor again. "Thanks, friend," he said over his shoulder. "But what made you help two people who, for all you know, could be murderers or spies or both?"

The thin man smiled, folding his features into a shape that lent his face a birdlike look. "Whenever authority is being defied," he said easily, "one likes to offer what help one can."

"But who are you?" This was Ingrid. "What are you doing here?"

He glanced down at the wide lapel of his trench coat. According to the badge pinned there, he was a systems analyst from Wroclaw in Poland. "Let us just say...a friend in need."

"Do you know how far it is to the nearest militia HQ

or military air base?" Bolan asked from the driving seat.

"Sumy. A little over forty miles to the northeast," the "Pole" offered.

"Then we have fifteen minutes to get rid of this buggy and lose ourselves," Bolan said. "If they are in direct radio contact, the choppers could be in the air already."

"If I may make a suggestion. . . ." the thin man said.

"Uh-huh." Bolan was racing the damaged coach toward the small town beyond the factory. According to the signs it was called Lubny. If they were lucky they might get through it before any military vehicles were called out.

"Your best bet is to make for the hills." The thin man gestured toward a low wooded ridge two or three miles to the south. "The trees will give you a certain amount of cover. But the road leading there is behind us: we passed it before we came to the factory. If you turn back now and take it without driving through town, they'll know at once that is the way you went. There is no alternative. If you go straight through Lubny, there is a track on the far side that doubles back through fields and orchards to join the hill road higher up. That way they will know from the townsfolk that you passed through. . . but there are several alternatives on the other side."

Bolan glanced over his shoulder. "I'll do that," he said. "Thanks, friend."

"It might give you as much as an extra quarter hour if you get to those trees quickly enough," the thin man said.

The town was gray and deserted. Drab two-story buildings stood in rows; tankers and container trucks sat among frozen puddles and rutted slush in a treeless parking lot next to a refinery, ramparts of dirty snow buttressed the sidewalks.

The track led between huge tin-roofed barns and a complex of grain silos half a mile farther on. "If you would just let me off here," the thin man said, "I'd be obliged."

Bolan stared at him. What the hell kind of joke was this? "Let you *off?*" he echoed.

"I cannot explain now, but I have a vehicle near here, just a couple of hundred yards away."

Bolan shrugged, punched the button that actuated the hydraulic door and slowed as he made the turn. The stranger stood up. For a moment he remained poised on the lowest step.

"Thanks for the ride," he called. "Goodbye, Professor Korsun. And good luck to you both." He raised a hand in salute and dropped lithely from the step. In the rearview mirror, Bolan saw him walking back toward the highway.

"Hell!" the Executioner exploded. "What do you make of that?"

"He knew my name," the woman said soberly.

"He could have seen you around the university. Your picture in the paper, maybe?"

"There has been no press coverage of my work. And how could he have seen me at the university? He just arrived. According to the identification on his lapel he was from Wroclaw in Poland."

"I don't think he's Polish," Bolan said decidedly.

"Then one must suppose he is here as illegally as you are. But why should he be here? Who can he be?"

Bolan shook his head. "Search me. Someone to help us along the way."

"Yes," Ingrid said. "And by the way. . . *which* way? How do you plan to make Odessa from here?"

The bus swerved on the icy track. They were passing rows of skeletal trees in what looked like a limitless orchard. Bolan had half turned in the driving seat.

"Odessa?"

She had taken over the Intourist position just behind him. "To get to Albania. Surely that is the best way? Once we are on the Black Sea it is plain sailing all the way down to the Dardanelles, the Straits of Marmora and the Aegean. From there we can either go over the mountains from Salonika or continue around Greece into the Adriatic."

Bolan braked and stamped on the kick-down to coax the Volga across the frozen surface of a ford. With half the window glass missing, even with the heaters at full blast it was penetratingly cold inside the coach. "Plain sailing?" he repeated.

"Otherwise we have to go through Romania, Bulgaria and Yugoslavia. Four frontiers to cross. Besides," she said, "that was the way we agreed."

"Odessa is just about the most heavily guarded naval base in history. The Black Sea and the straits are not exactly free of patrol boats. I wouldn't take you within fifty miles of Odessa unless I had a miniature submarine equipped with radar, mine detectors and a nuclear torpedo tube."

"It was agreed that this was the best route," Ingrid said stubbornly. "They told me they had found a fool-proof way—"

"Maybe you didn't understand before," Bolan snapped. "*I'm* telling you. And I'm the one responsible for getting you out. Those arrangements were not foolproof. There was a leak somewhere. So that plan, like the others, is bitched."

Ingrid compressed her lips and lapsed into silence.

"We'll take the route I choose, at the time I decide," Bolan said tightly.

Yeah, he thought grimly as he assessed their situation. Big deal. So who's talking? A guy whose cover was only good for the city he just quit; a foreigner who snatched a highly prized morsel of Soviet property and now found himself three hundred miles inside Russia with assets of one Tokarev automatic with an empty magazine and one army-issue Stechkin machine pistol with a full one.

And on the debit side, the KGB and half the Red Army's southern command are after him.

Add so far as the property was concerned he was nothing more than a con man, an impostor. And she was likely to be mad as hell when she found out.

Blueprint for a happy journey, Bolan thought. See the wintry delights of rural Ukraine from the panoramic viewing deck of our windowless bus. Special on this one trip: a close-up of Red Army maneuvers.

He shrugged. What the hell: he had trod the unfamiliar jungle of Vietnam before, where each tree, each bush was a potential lurking enemy; he'd been boxed in by the killer hordes of the U.S. Mafia, much to their chagrin, to put it mildly. And he'd come up against a far superior adversary than the Mob—the same one he was dodging now, the KGB—and survived. Sure they were assassins, saboteurs and murderers. But they did not have *this* soldier's instincts, his determination, indeed, his *personal* will to win.

They had left the track for a country road that arrowed toward the hills. He had used up twelve minutes of the fifteen he had allowed himself before the road began twisting upward through dense birch woods whose bare branches stood black against the pale sky. If the mysterious stranger had been right, they might have another quarter of an hour.

So far they had passed two produce trucks and a rusted Moskvitch sedan, all heading downhill for Lubny. Through two small villages, apart from shaggy-coated peasants chopping logs beneath the overhanging eaves of their wooden shacks, they had seen no human activity. For a time a bright yellow pickup with heavy-duty tires trailed them, but once the road narrowed and the surface began to deteriorate they left it behind.

Bolan was pushing the coach all he dared. Seventeen minutes after they left the factory, Ingrid broke her silence. "There is something following us, I believe," she said. "You cannot see it all the time because the route is too twisty, but I think it may be an army vehicle. In any case it is going faster than we are."

The road was spiraling now through a pine forest. Bolan was able to glance only occasionally at the driving mirror. Already through gaps in the trees he could see white peaks in the distance. Behind—yes, finally he caught it—a dun shape, no, two, on a loop of road below.

A Red Army scout car, a Czech-built Tatra with a heavy machine gun mounted beside the driver. Behind it was a flatter shape, an armored personnel carrier, its slewing tracks flailing mud and snow from the banks on each corner.

Bolan set his teeth and concentrated on the controls. It was difficult to urge the wide, heavy coach to make more than forty miles per hour on such a hilly, narrow and sinuous route. The APC and the Tatra would be able to push at least fifty on the short straightaways. There would be four soldiers in the scout car and anything up to twelve behind the steel screens of the APC, armed with Kalashnikovs and possibly RPG-7 grenade launchers.

Taking them out was going to be a lot of work for one Stechkin machine pistol.

"At least they will not shoot while they believe I am with you," the woman said. "It will be important for them to keep me alive."

"Think they'll know you wrecked the computer?"

"Perhaps."

"If they do," Bolan said, "then they'll also know that you wished to leave. If not...well, I could have taken you against your will. It makes a difference."

She opened her mouth to reply—and then caught her breath. An enormous trailer truck stacked high with lumber hurtled around a corner fifty yards ahead of them and bore down on the bus with frightening speed, snaking on the slippery roadway. Bolan had to wrench at the wheel and send the Volga plowing through snow piled along the shoulder to avoid it.

But the near miss gave him an idea. He pushed the speed up higher still, rocketing the coach from side to side. Two more curves and he found what he wanted—a roadside clearing where loggers had been at work, the wide space still covered with half-frozen snow.

Ingrid gasped as he drove straight off the road. He kicked down again, wheels scrabbling over the rough ground, and then when the nearest line of trees was dangerously close, he braked fiercely, hauled on the hand brake to lock the rear wheels and swung the steering hard over.

The coach spun, shuddering around in a half circle. Metal shrieked and glass splintered as the tail clipped the trunk of a tree. The vehicle tipped precariously half over before Bolan, fighting the wheel, was able to force it back onto the road, heading downhill now the way they had come. "Lie on the floor," he yelled at Ingrid, "and stay there."

The driver of the accelerating scout car, rounding a corner and expecting to see the rear of the coach disappearing beyond the next, found instead that the quarry was thundering straight down toward him.

For one fatal moment he hesitated.

The Tatra lost way, the driver lost control—and his life as well.

Bolan, using all his skill at the wheel combined with

the coach's weight and downhill speed, broadsided the heavy vehicle across the roadway in a controlled slide as he drew level with the scout car.

The coach's damaged tail flicked out, skated crazily across the grade and then swung in again to slam against the armored side of the Tatra between the front and rear wheels.

The scout car reared up like a terrified horse, hit the snowbank and toppled over into the ditch on the far side. The gas tank ruptured and ignited at once. Then the tank exploded, turning the scout car into a blazing fireball.

The soldier driving the APC struggled with levers and ran one of his tracks up on the bank to miss the skidding Volga.

Thirty yards behind him Bolan steered the bus off the road and slid it in a final broadside against the nearest trees, with the door facing away from the pursuers.

"Out!"

He grabbed the woman's arm and pulled her from the crumpled wreck. Glass was still falling; steam hissed from the tortured engine. "Drop behind those bushes, lie flat and don't move until I tell you."

Grasping the machine pistol he had taken from the dead militiaman inside the coach, he worked his way on elbows and knees through the undergrowth.

Uphill an officer and five men—not the full dozen he had feared—had leaped from the stalled APC. Two were carrying RPG-7s, three had Kalashnikovs and the officer was clutching a heavy caliber pistol.

Behind them a tall column of black smoke marbled with flame leaned in among the trees. The burning Tatra and its incinerated occupants had set fire to a row of pine saplings and these blazed like funeral torches on either side.

"Come out with your hands up, all three of you," the

officer shouted, "or we shall launch grenades and destroy the coach."

"They won't," Ingrid called to Bolan in a low voice. "They need me alive."

"I know." Bolan was still moving. "They will try tear gas or stun grenades. Keep your head down and turned away."

Did they know he had the dead Russian's gun? Probably. And they would certainly know about the Tokarev—although not that he was fresh out of ammunition for it.

The soldiers had deployed in a line behind the snowbank. The nearest was about twenty yards away. The officer was farthest. He had remained near the carrier.

The Russian officer barked a command. Each of the three men with the Kalashnikovs fitted an extension to the barrel of his weapon. Another order. The weapons spit fire.

Two stun grenades and a gas canister arced over the road and dropped through the glassless windows of the coach.

Even from where he lay Bolan felt the shock wave of the Slepoys. Smoke curled from the inside of the wreck.

The officer waved his men forward. They climbed from behind the bank and rushed toward the Volga.

Bolan raised the Stechkin, sighted carefully and squeezed the trigger.

A short burst.

The officer appeared to leap backward against the dun steel side of the carrier. He slid to the ground, transforming the red star painted on the metal into a wavering crimson smear.

The five men halted in midstride halfway across the road as soon as they heard Bolan fire. One, presumably an NCO, yelled a command. Two of the soldiers whirled and made for the snowbank. Two more kept going. The NCO, too, headed for the bank.

Bolan gunned down the pair running for the coach with another short burst, the MP's breechwork warm against his frozen hands. In the center of the road long streamers of blood stained Christmas patterns in the snow.

Bolan flattened himself and crawled away beneath the frosted leaves as the NCO opened fire on full auto with the remaining Kalashnikov. The steel-cored 7.62mm slugs thwacked through the branches above Bolan's head.

The Executioner knew he had to act quickly now. Two of the three assault rifles had been accounted for, but the remaining soldiers were the ones with the RPGs. If they got a fix on him, and realized he was separated from the woman, those HE rocket grenades could end the action with a single exchange.

Suddenly, fire streaked the air with an express-train roar as one of the men launched his shoulder-borne rocket.

The grenade burst with a livid flash, an eruption of brown smoke, only a few yards from where Bolan had zapped the officer. Chunks of iron-hard earth whistled through the trees, showering his back with painful fragments. A second shell exploded, sending splinters of wood spinning.

Another idea came to Bolan. The soldiers behind the snowbank were sheltered by the overhanging branches of fir trees. The branches drooped low, heavy with snow.

Once again he took careful aim.

The MP hammered out a brief message—upward into the firs.

Branches threshed. The snowload slithered, fell.

The blanket of white thumped softly down, blinding the Russians in a pale cloud, knocking one to the ground. Bolan was on his feet in the center of the roadway, spewing death from the squat weapon between his hands.

Through smoke condensing in the subzero air he saw the ghosts of gunmen, struggling white flecked with red, subsiding to the muddied, ice-cold earth.

A stammer of shots sighed overhead and Bolan dropped to one knee, finger tightening on the trigger and snout acquiring target on the NCO and his assault rifle.

Click.

An empty magazine and Bolan was a bull's-eye. But several shots rang out now from behind, leaving the last Russian with his boots pointing skyward on top of the snowbank, his body a huddle of stained garments in the ditch.

Ingrid Korsun had crawled to one of the dead riflemen and taken possession of his gun.

Bolan had collected all the weapons, feeling secure for the first time since he crossed the border. There was a large-scale map of the area netted above the driving seat of the Volga, and they had taken that too.

The only problem had been the unconscious driver himself.

Bolan had bound him with soldiers' belts, fashioned a gag with strips torn from a shirt and left him between two seats. Bolan was sure the man wouldn't freeze before he was found.

Outside the shattered windows, Bolan had faced the woman. "Coming originally from the Baltic, you don't speak Polish, do you?"

"But of course."

"Fine. Most of the folks around here do too. Lvov, on the far side of Kiev, used to be a Polish town."

She had stared at him in puzzlement.

Bolan said: "Come into the bus. We're going to lay a little false trail on the guy. Here's what I want you to say—in Polish."

She nodded and they climbed the steps.

"We must leave now," Ingrid said in Polish. "It will soon be night and there is a lot of ground to cover if we are to make contact near Lvov before dawn."

As Bolan had surmised, the driver was regaining consciousness, moaning faintly behind the gag.

Bolan flashed a sideways glance. A flicker of intelligence and understanding had shown for an instant in the driver's eyes. Then the lids closed again in feigned coma as Ingrid continued: "After that we shall be all right. The Dniester is shallow there and the Niva they have waiting for us is built very high. If we take the dirt road that crosses the Jaroslaw-Przemyzl highway...."

Between each sentence that Ingrid spoke Bolan had allowed his voice to sink to an unintelligible mumble.

With luck, when the man was found he would report that the fugitives were heading west for Poland.

With luck.

They had made it through the woods in the APC. The machine had left unmistakable tracks on the forest floor but they could do nothing about that.

The carrier churned its way southward, toward the higher ground. The sky above the treetops darkened and it began to snow once more. But this time icy winds from the steppes dried the flakes into tiny particles that whirled like white sand between the branches and stung their faces raw in the open-sided APC.

It was almost dark when Bolan decided it would be foolish to go farther. More foolish still to show lights, even over uninhabited terrain like this. They had found a stony forest trail that zigzagged in roughly the direction he wished to go. In a hollow that offered shelter from the wind's whine, they came to an abandoned sawmill and pulled in beneath its sagging roof for the night. If they were not flushed out before morning, Bolan told the woman, they would junk the carrier and make it another way.

Fifteen minutes before, they had heard the rotor throb of choppers circling the site of the firefight.

HE'S EXPLOSIVE. HE'S MACK BOLAN... AGAINST ALL ODDS

He learned his deadly skills in Vietnam...then put them to good use by destroying the Mafia in a blazing one-man war. Now **Mack Bolan** ventures further into the cold to take on his deadliest challenge yet—the KGB's worldwide terror machine.

Follow the lone warrior on his exciting new missions...and get ready for more nonstop action from his high-powered combat teams: **Able Team**—Bolan's famous Death Squad—battling urban savagery too brutal and volatile for regular law enforcement. And **Phoenix Force**—five extraordinary warriors handpicked by Bolan to fight the dirtiest of antiterrorist wars, blazing into even greater danger.

Fight alongside these three courageous forces for freedom in all-new action-packed novels! Travel to the gloomy depths of the cold Atlantic, the scorching sands of the Sahara, and the desolate Russian plains. You'll feel the pressure and excitement building page after page, with nonstop action that keeps you enthralled until the explosive conclusion!

Now you can have all the new Gold Eagle novels delivered right to your home!

You won't want to miss a single one of these exciting new action-adventures. And you don't have to! Just fill out and mail the card at right, and we'll enter your name in the Gold Eagle home subscription plan. You'll then receive six brand-new action-packed Gold Eagle books every other month, delivered right to your home! You'll get two Mack Bolan novels, one Able Team and one Phoenix Force, plus one book each from two thrilling, new Gold Eagle libraries, **SOBs** and **Track**. In **SOBs** you'll meet the legendary team of mercenary warriors who fight for justice and win. **Track** features a military and weapons genius on a mission to stop a maniac whose dream is everybody's worst nightmare. Only Track stands between us and nuclear hell!

FREE! The New War Book and Mack Bolan bumper sticker.

As soon as we receive your card we'll rush you the long-awaited New War Book and Mack Bolan bumper sticker—both ABSOLUTELY FREE with your first six Gold Eagle novels.

The New War Book is *packed* with exciting information for Bolan fans: a revealing look at the hero's life...two new short stories...book character biographies...even a combat catalog describing weapons used in the novels! The New War Book is a special collector's item you'll want to read again and again. And it's yours FREE when you mail your card!

Of course, you're under no obligation to buy anything. Your first six books come on a 10-day free trial—if you're not thrilled with them, just return them and owe nothing. The New War Book and bumper sticker are yours to keep, FREE!

Don't miss a single one of these thrilling novels...mail the card now, while you're thinking about it.

13

Greb Strakhov was angry. The flat planes of his face flared a remarkable red. The strutting footsteps as he stamped up and down his office in the yellow sandstone building in Kiev shook the walls. When he spoke, his voice rasped many decibels louder than his normal measured tones.

Three KGB section chiefs, a man from the Kiev MVD directorate, together with the local militia commandant and Colonel Antonin stood pale-faced and quailing before his wrath.

"You had him there. You had him!" Strakhov raged. "Yet with all available manpower of the state at your disposal, with all the advantages on your side, you let him go. It is unbelievable."

"Comrade General, there were certain unforeseen circumstances," the MVD man began.

"Silence! He was known to be in the city. I myself had seen him. He is not a nonentity, a man over two meters high. With a limp." Strakhov's fury turned to scorn. "But still you missed him at the university, you missed him at the exhibition palace, you allowed him to knock one of your guards unconscious and run rings around the others. Then to cap it all, after you have kindly permitted him to leave the city, he is located at a scheduled factory one hour's drive away...and still you are unable to lay hands on him."

"He had contrived to find himself a believable cover

identity as a trade fair delegate, comrade General,'' the militia chief said.

"A delegate?'' Strakhov screamed. "There are two thousand foreigners circulating at the fair. Half of them are women. Of the thousand who remain, how many are more than two meters tall? And how many of that small minority walk with a limp, tell me that?''

"So far as the noncommissioned officer at the factory was concerned, it was no more than a routine check until—''

"Until the criminal sought by the whole of Kiev murders two of his men and makes off with a coach—a piece of government property—and the woman scientist he has kidnapped.''

"Comrade General,'' Antonin daringly interposed, "it is not certain that the woman Korsun was kidnapped. According to some reports it was she, alone, who obtained the tickets for the trip. Other witnesses speak of an attack she herself made on the driver of the coach.''

"Rubbish. Witnesses are notoriously unreliable. Doubtless she was trying vainly to protect the comrade driver from the murderous assault launched by this foreign jackal. She would never willingly accompany such a man. She has the Order of Lenin.''

"Several of my agents,'' the militia chief said, "report a third person involved in the fight within the coach. What appeared to be another delegate is said to have joined in on the foreigner's side.''

"An invention to distract attention from their own inefficiency. As for you—'' Strakhov turned to the three KGB men "—you have half a dozen helicopters at your disposal within minutes of the assault, and it takes you one hour to locate the coach—empty. The surrounding woods, however, are full of slaughtered soldiers.''

"The foreigner was astute, comrade General,'' one of

the operatives ventured. "He made good use of the woods. We were not at first able to see—"

"You could not see the nose in front of your stupid face," Strakhov shouted. "It is clear that I shall have to take charge of this operation personally, in the area where the criminal was last seen. Why am I continually surrounded by fools who cannot be trusted to carry out the simplest of tasks?"

Nobody was prepared to answer this question. A second KGB agent said, "With respect, comrade General, the coach was not entirely empty. There was a survivor, the driver himself, and he has information of the fugitives' plans. . . ."

"Which evidently requires the intervention of a trained mind," Strakhov said sarcastically, "in order that this information is not misinterpreted and yet another blunder made." He strode to the door. "That is why I am taking charge myself. We shall leave at once for Lubny. You, Antonin, you, Zhukov—" to the MVD official "—and you, Kopalsky. Since it is the members of your militia who have been mainly instrumental in allowing this intruder to escape, you three will accompany me."

He surveyed each of the six men with a cold eye. "You would do well to remember, all of you, that dereliction of duty is a serious crime against the Party and the State. . . and that there is always a demand for more workers in the labor camps beyond the Urals."

He flung open the door and headed for the elevators. There was a helipad on the roof of the KGB building, with two WSK Swidniks on constant alert. Strakhov commandeered one. Three minutes later the jet recon ship was slicing through flurries of fresh falling snow toward the east and the dark.

CIRCLING OVER LUBNY, the thrashing rotors of the Swidnik could be heard clearly by two men sitting in an unheated dacha in the pinewoods above the vast Krementchoug reservoir. In summer the windows of the dacha overlooked the northern arm of the lake, where the waters of the Psël and Uday rivers flowed into the drowned valley of the Dnieper. But now the shutters were closed, no light burned and snow had almost covered the bicycle tracks that led to the building from a nearby forest trail.

The two men welcomed the winter weather. Since their visit was secret, they were marooned in the dacha, blocked until the snow melted away or kept falling fast enough to obliterate their tracks when they left.

The older of the two was stocky and swarthy, with a Zapata mustache. His name was Frank Santayana, a delegate to the trade fair, and a genuine one: although his passport was Mexican, he represented several South American and Third World countries that were anxious to study the latest Soviet agricultural machinery.

Philippe Peller had come to the Ukraine on a very minor diplomatic mission, representing the French government at the opening session of the convention that formed part of the fair. He was a thin, balding, saturnine forty-year-old who wore heavy shell-rimmed spectacles.

Undercover, both men worked for the Central Intelligence Agency, Santayana as a field agent, Peller as secret assistant to the Paris resident.

"That will be the second wave, trying to locate them," Peller observed when the sound of the helicopter became audible. "I guess they screwed up with the first. Mister Big could be heading this way in person. According to the grapevine the guy doesn't exactly carry a torch for Bolan."

"I'll take your word for it," Santayana said. "Can't we light those logs now?" He nodded toward the cavernous fireplace. "It's cold enough to freeze your balls off in here. Why the hell did we have to trail out to this place anyway? On *bicycles*!''

"Orders were that we were to meet only in a safe house, and this was the nearest. It's a permitted summer residence for our dipcorps people in Moscow. Off limits in winter—which is why we are here. At this time of year nobody's listening in. We can have a fire as soon as the snow's falling thickly enough to hide the smoke."

"Couldn't we have met someplace in Kiev?"

Peller shook his head. "We can't afford to be seen talking together. Even if they hadn't chosen to make that factory tour, we might still have had to come here. It's not one hundred percent certain that I'm clean, you see. As a third-rank French diplomat I'm automatically suspect, anyway. And they may have cottoned on to the U.S. connection in Paris. You never know." He shook his head again. "What it cost me, shaking my tail and making the coach in the city!"

"Yeah. Being Third World, I don't have to mess with that," Santayana said. "But what about this guy and the bus? This sonofabitch Bolan! Turns up from no-place, puts the broad in the bag and then knocks off a coupla cops and hijacks the bus, cool as you please."

"The girl seemed to pack a punch too, leaving us there staring, the Intourist *nana* screaming blue murder and the soldier boys all playing Fourth of July." Peller sighed. "What bugs me though is who the hell was number three? The dude left in the bus with them, the delegate who joined in and delivered the final kayo."

Santayana shrugged. "Your guess is as good as mine. All I know is, I was told to bring this broad in at any cost. They always feed you this need-to-know shit at Langley." He chuckled. "But the DOD sure are hot on the idea of this chick and her super computer. They can't wait to get their hands on her. Tell me, pal, how did they fit you into the scenario?"

"We discovered that the comrades had a wiretap on a house in Paris, and we figured we'd like to know why. So we spike-miked the outer walls of their safe house and listened in to the playbacks."

Peller walked to a window, pushed open a shutter and looked out at the whirling snow. The sky was a sulfurous yellow and daylight was vanishing fast. "I guess we could light that fire now," he said. "The Russkis knew there was to be a penetration. Where and when. But they didn't know the target area and they didn't know the aim of the operation."

"But we did?"

"We cross-checked every way. A Yugoslav mole planted in Tirana, Albania, came up with the connecting link—a Soviet electronics expert in Kiev wanted to defect to the Chinese. It was only by chance that we realized the penetration agent was Bolan. Some guy once knew him spotted him leaving that house in Paris."

"Check," Santayana said. He was on his hands and knees by the piled logs, a matchbox in his hand. "And the routine now?"

"Bolan has the girl. Presumably it's some kind of hijack or con. She was expecting an Albanian. Point is, he has her. So we let him run with the ball, taking over when he's nearer the frontier and it'll be easier for us."

"But we already lost him," Santayana objected. "We don't—"

"No sweat. We have a list of all the contacts he's been given, the places he must go on the way out. We can afford to let it ride, catch up someplace along the way."

"They never told me that. They never tell me *anything*," Santayana complained bitterly. The wood was damp. He struck his seventh match. "How come?"

"A local Moldavian. He'd been turned by the folks hiring Bolan. What they didn't know was that he was also working for us. Guy named Schelgatseff. We'd hoped to get more details in the field, but the opposition got to him first.''

"Who *are* the folks hiring this Bolan anyway?"

"Civilians. Emigré anticoms. God knows what they want with the girl. Sell her to the highest bidder maybe? If she's ready to be sold, which I doubt. Nutcases anyway, but rich. So we let them make the running until we're good and ready. Then we step in and play hard ball.''

"And Bolan? Where does he fit in?"

"He doesn't." Peller adjusted his spectacles and permitted himself a faint smile, almost a grimace. "According to the latest service messages, your friends at Langley wouldn't be too unhappy if Bolan met with an accident. Not even if it was fatal.''

"You mean 'Terminate with extreme prejudice'?''

"Not that hard. There's no contract out. But to lay it on you straight, as far as the Company is concerned Mack Bolan is expendable.''

THE THIN MAN who had helped Bolan and the woman during the brief battle in the bus parked the bright yellow Pobeda pickup with heavy-duty tires in a clearing not far from the abandoned sawmill.

It was appallingly cold.

In the dusk the snow fell thickly, the biting Siberian wind driving gray-white flakes hard against the sides of the canvas-topped utility, rustling dryly against the taut material, clinging to the windshield and the flexible plastic sideglasses.

He was used to hardships, but this bone-chilling cold numbed him from head to foot and slowed the beating of his heart to a dangerous degree. Nor could he use the heater, inefficient though it was: the sound of the engine was a risk he dared not take. Not yet. Not tonight.

He wrapped his fur-lined *tchouba* as closely about

him as he could and settled down in the passenger seat to spend what he knew would be an uncomfortable night. Every hour he took a sip from a flask of vodka to keep his circulation alive.

Next to the flask in the glove compartment was a Walther P5 automatic. Several times during the long night he unloaded and reloaded the eight 9mm shells into the magazine with frozen fingers. Finally he pulled back the slide to charge the breech and snapped on the safety.

He knew he was going to need that pistol sometime the next day. And he might need to use it in a hurry.

14

Bolan and the woman, too, spent an uncomfortable night. Neither of them had eaten since early that morning and the intense cold seemed to sharpen the pangs of hunger they suffered. There was no question of remaining on the metal seats of the carrier. The wind howled in through the open sides of the lean-to, and although the abandoned mill was in a hollow, it was still strong enough to stir up occasional clouds of sawdust mingled with icy flakes of driven snow.

Above the rusted machinery in the main body of the mill there was a gallery with an office at one end that was reached via a rickety ladder. The glass had gone from the windows and there were no chairs, but Bolan had rigged a shelter from an old table and a tarpaulin he found in the APC. Beneath this, huddled together for warmth, their backs resting against a wall, they passed the hours of darkness.

Even through the thick winter garments, Bolan was aware of Ingrid Korsun's sexuality and her animal vitality. But he dismissed any thoughts of capitalizing on this as part of a plan to incline her toward the West.

They had been through a lot together. Yet he hardly knew her. He had no idea what made her tick. He was ignorant of her feelings, her mental makeup, her character. She was a mystery.

At least, he figured, he could make a start by talking. Because she had to be won over within the next few days.

He found the task hard going.

After a few routine questions about her work, he said, "It makes me sad, all this shooting. I have nothing against the Russian people. I hope you realize that under the circumstances I have no choice."

"I come from Estonia," she reminded him. "I am neither Russian nor Ukrainian. Why should I mind?"

"Did you find a great difference—in the way folks live, I mean—when you first left Estonia and moved to Russia?"

"No."

"Will it mean a great change in your social life, leaving the Soviet Union and going to China?"

"The true scientist, the seeker after truth, has no social life."

Three strikes and out. Bolan relapsed into silence.

She was slumped with her head against his shoulder, supported by his arm, but she was unrelaxed, her body stiff, her manner distant. "Have you been to Albania before?" he asked later.

He felt her shake her head.

"My brief ends when I get you to the capital," he said, still trying to make conversation. "You knew all the details of the route we should have taken if there had been no leak here. Have you any idea how you'll make it from Tirana to Peking?"

"No," she said. "Not yet."

"I guess you're excited by the thought."

"It is simply something that has to be done."

"But the conditions will make for better work, won't they?"

"Bureaucracy and self-interest have sullied the communist ideal in this country. There, it is to be hoped, ethics are more highly prized."

"Do you think life for the workers in China has become easier since the so-called cultural revolution?"

"Perhaps. It is not for me to say."

Despairingly, Bolan tried another tack. "How long will it take you to rebuild the RIAMS computer?"

For the first time her voice was colored with enthusiasm. "It depends, of course," she said, "on the skills available, on the quality of assistance at my disposal and on the number of technicians involved who will be familiar with my methods of notation. With the maximum help it should be possible to reconstruct, even improve the system within a year. With minimal help it could take two or three."

Bolan realized he wasn't having much success with the woman. He fell silent.

After some moments she spoke again. "What interests me most right now is the route you plan to follow from here to Tirana."

"I'll tell you tomorrow when you can follow it on the map," he said.

Eventually they fell into an uneasy sleep.

DAYLIGHT WAS NO MORE THAN A HINT of yellow filtering through the branches when Bolan started the diesel motor of the personnel carrier. Although the wind had dropped before dawn and the snow was falling less thickly, it was still shudderingly cold. The chill pierced through leather, fur and wool to the bone, numbing his fingers, nose and ears, bringing tears to his eyes. Outside the mill the snow was almost knee-deep.

He wasn't going to tell the woman, but he figured on crossing the Dnieper between the Krementchoug reservoir and a smaller lake upstream, bypassing the towns of Cherkassy and Smela and then traversing the higher ground that separated the Dnieper basin from Vinnitsa. That far, he could still believably be trying to make Poland. And the upper stretches of the Dniester, which figured in the scenario they had laid on the bus driver, still lay ahead.

If the pursuers tracked him that far, okay. It should

mean that their attempt to block him would be deployed between Vinnitsa and the Polish border. But Bolan's plan was to turn south once he reached the Dniester valley and race for the Carpathian foothills near the Romanian border.

Hopefully the duchess's Gypsies would be waiting for him at Solca, a mountain village a few miles on the far side of the frontier. They were to pass Bolan and his companion through to Yugoslavia, where arrangements had been made to graft them onto a winter sports package tour returning to Italy.

Provided that Bolan had come clean, revealed his true identity and persuaded Ingrid that West was best.

He dismissed the idea. There was no point even thinking about it until closer, more urgent problems had been faced.

For one thing, as he had told her, they would have to junk the carrier the moment they emerged from the woods on the far side of the ridge and find alternative transport. With the hue and cry that must have been raised by now, it would be suicide to remain in a stolen military vehicle, especially in civilian clothes.

Apart from that, it would be physically almost impossible. The APC had been called out in a hurry. It had not been prepared for snow patrol: no side screens, no canvas top, nothing to protect their faces from the icy blast whistling through the slit in the armor, the stinging flakes sucked down from the blizzard above.

They passed nothing and nobody but two men wheeling bicycles through the drifts.

The trees were thinning out. Between squalls Bolan surveyed the wide valley immediately below them, webbed with a network of snowbound minor roads barely distinguishable from the squares of cultivation between them. Their pace had slowed to a near-blind crawl and the tracks were churning up clouds of white before Bolan heard the unmistakable clatter-whine of a jet chopper over the roar of the diesel.

At first he could make out nothing. Then he saw three helicopters, two of them skimming the snowfields at hedge height.

The third was searching the edge of the forest, cruising on a zigzag vector that would bring it almost directly overhead in another half dozen passes.

Bolan rocked the carrier to a halt. No traffic punctuated the snow-covered roads that crisscrossed the white wilderness below. The APC was going to stand out like a blip on a radar screen once the Swidnik was near enough for its navigator's eyes to penetrate the flurries.

Bolan flashed a quick glance behind. Fifty yards away where the trail ran between steep banks, skeletons of last year's brambles arched over the track's edge to form a short tunnel roofed with white. Beneath that arch they would be invisible from the air.

"Quick! Make for it." Bolan pointed. "And take these."

In the troop-carrying section of the vehicle, the arms they had commandeered were stacked beneath the tarp. Two grenade launchers, three assault rifles, a Stechkin MP and the Tokarev pistol that had belonged to the officer in charge of the patrol.

Bolan handed Ingrid the pistol, a Kalashnikov, two spare box magazines and a rocket grenade that he unclipped from a rack beside the codriver's seat. She staggered away through the calf-high snow.

He followed seconds later with two more grenades, an RPG-7 launcher and another assault rifle. Fortunately the Tokarev pistol was the same model as his own empty automatic and there were spare clips for these too. He stuffed them along with the map into his pockets.

The ground beneath the briar shelter was frozen hard.

Bolan squatted beside the woman, fitting one of the grenades to the launch tube.

The noise of the Swidnik's rotors was loud now over the moan of the wind. An amplified voice, muffled by the snow, shouted something unintelligible through a bullhorn.

Soon through the entrance to their refuge they could make out a dragonfly shape hovering over the abandoned carrier. Bolan had no idea whether their tracks would be visible from that height or whether the crew might stay at a respectful distance, thinking they were still aboard.

Bolan watched the helicopter standing off, taking no risks. Both blister hatches were open, a guy standing in each behind a flex-mounted heavy machine gun.

As the chopper veered left and then right with the pilot's efforts to counteract the wind, each gunner poured down a scalding hail of lead at the APC. The belts were obviously fitted with the classic airfighters' mix alternating HE, incendiary and armor-piercing rounds.

The Executioner saw the tracer slice through the snowstorm, stitching the carrier to the ground. Then fire winked briefly from the launch pods beneath the Swidnik's stub wings. Two S-5 rockets leaped from the pods, streaking earthward to hammer the tracked vehicle with a double burst.

Orange flames veined with brown transformed the APC into a boiling fireball. A length of caterpillar track torn off by the explosions lashed through the air like a wounded snake. Then the white heat detonated the remainder of the ammunition stashed inside. There was a rippling roar as the grenades erupted one after the other, crumpling armor plate, throwing off spinning fireballs that trailed spirals of smoke through the storm. Finally the small-arms magazines discharged, peppering the early morning with firecracker volleys.

Flame licked the blackened molten remains of the carrier. The Swidnik hovered, then landed in a field eighty yards from the roadway.

Billows of powdered snow stirred up by the rotor wash momentarily obscured Bolan's view. Then he saw that three men had fanned out from the ship and were advancing toward the road. A fourth stood in the hatch behind one of the machine guns.

Bolan couldn't tell if they had been spotted from the air. The tracks leading from the carrier to the shelter would certainly be visible as soon as the Russians reached the road.

Bolan knew he had to act quickly. Had they radioed the other two helicopters for help as soon as they located the APC? Or were they waiting for the kill? In any case the pall of smoke over the guttering wreck would attract the others' attention and bring them over pretty damned quick.

Bolan hoisted the RPG-7 onto his shoulder. There was a blast of flame, a thudding explosion as the missile was percussion-fired, and then the rocket motor ignited, the fins opened and the grenade streaked for the Swidnik. It burst ten yards short of the ship, showering it with frozen clods of earth.

He seized another projectile, fitted it and fired again.

This time he scored a direct hit just behind the blister. There was a blinding flash. The tail assembly broke away, the rotors canted forward and dug into the snow. The cabin was transformed into an inferno of twisted metal and liquefied Plexiglas. The explosion when it reached them was deadened by the snow.

The three attackers had dropped out of sight the moment the RPG-7 was fired. Were they armed with Kalashnikovs? Bolan guessed the weapons would be slung over their backs while they wormed their way invisibly through the snow.

By now they would have separated too far to be zapped as a unit. He had to neutralize each one individually and get the hell out before they reached positions from which they could outflank his refuge.

Before they were close enough to lob a hand grenade.

Before the other two choppers showed.

The bank protected the hiding place, but it also stopped Bolan sighting the enemy without exposing himself. The bank was an impasse.

He loaded the last grenade and handed the tube to the woman. "There's a hell of a kick to this," he said, "but don't be afraid. Hold these two grips, one in each hand. The trigger's in front of the forward grip. Sight through the eyepiece and aim anyplace between here and the chopper. You won't hit anything but it'll make a diversion I may be able to use."

Ingrid nodded and took the weapon.

"Fire when I give the signal," he told her. Grabbing the pistol and one of the rifles he crawled rapidly back along their own tracks to the burned-out carrier. There was no bank there, just the snow piled up along the shoulder. Shielded by smoke still eddying from the tangle of scorched steel, he rose cautiously to his knees.

Snowflakes hissed on the hot metal. One third of the way between the chopper and the bank he could see marks, darker brushstrokes across the white snowfield. He waved to the woman.

The last round of the RPG-7 cracked out, followed an instant later by the duller roar of the bursting grenade.

Beyond the smoke flash, Bolan saw movement. A threshing of limbs, a dark stirring of the field's bright surface. By chance Ingrid's grenade had also scored a hit.

Farther away another figure rose upright among the whirling flakes. An arm drew back in the classic grenadier's stance. The Russian was aiming for the lip of the bank where the launcher had flamed.

Bolan seized the Kalashnikov. He fired a single shot, dropping the man and the bomb, which exploded a moment later, splashing the snow with scarlet.

Two down and one to go.

The last man was on his feet now farther away, approaching the trail from behind the shelter. And Bolan saw that he had been mistaken: he was armed not with an assault rifle but a Suomi SMG.

He took a chance. The Russian was perhaps 130 yards away, and the AK-74's range was more than three times that.

But the accurate effective range of the Suomi, firing pistol ammunition, was barely one hundred yards.

Bolan stepped into the center of the trail, shoving the stiff selector lever onto automatic. Three shots ripped out in rapid succession were enough to draw the guy's attention away from the woman. The Executioner fired from the hip at the distant figure half hidden by falling snow. The shots fell wide and short.

Bolan sighted just above the pinpoint of light flickering at the weapon's muzzle and blazed off another short burst. The AK's deathstream lashed the Russian across the chest and hurled him lifeless to the side of the road.

The Executioner ran for the shelter. For some time he had been aware of two sounds, each increasing steadily in volume: the whine of the wind and the approaching racket of the other two choppers.

Now suddenly the wind was increasing to gale force, blowing the fast-falling snow almost horizontally across the open fields.

In such blizzard conditions the Swidnik crews would be able to see nothing on the ground. They would be forced to either land or try to rise above the storm. And even if they landed, they would be no threat: the light was fading, visibility was fast reducing to a few yards.

Bolan forced his way back to the woman. "This is our

chance to make it," he panted. "We'll go back to the woods and choose another exit when the storm is over."

Turning up collars and ducking their heads, they battled half blinded against the freezing crystals assaulting their eyes, mouths and noses until they reached the partial shelter of the trees.

15

Bolan and Ingrid Korsun were crouched behind a screen of bushes at the edge of the forest, five or six miles north of the trail where Bolan had annihilated the helicopter and its crew.

It was late afternoon and the racing clouds drew suddenly apart to reveal an oasis of blue sky. Brittle winter sunshine splashed patches of brilliance across the glittering white landscape below.

The snow had stopped falling an hour before.

Throughout the day they had been aware of the sounds of pursuit: a grinding of gears, the whirring of tracked vehicles, sometimes a distant voice dehumanized by a loudspeaker, distorted with static, bawling incomprehensible orders. On several occasions they had heard the approach of helicopter patrols.

But their flight under cover, within the fringes of the wood, had never been challenged directly. Slowly they had made their way, keeping as far as possible to the areas where interlaced branches had prevented the snow from falling thickly enough to lie, to a spur from which they could overlook the valley.

Now, each of them armed with the Kalashnikov, the pistol and the spare clips that were all they had salvaged from the decimated carrier, they surveyed the terrain they would have to cross.

"The militia have control points on all main roads outside big cities like Kiev," Ingrid said. "I expect you know that. But after last night and this morning they are going to be everywhere, on every road, especially around here.''

"Check," Bolan said. "Some of them are down there now." He gestured toward the thread of highway that followed the lower contours of the valley. There were fewer tracks leading off it here: the slope was too steep for cultivation. As far as they could see the terrain was mainly scrub beneath the snow. But along the road the antlike column of men, the small convoy of military vehicles, were clearly visible against the white.

"How are we going to get to the other side of the valley and then over the far hill?" the woman asked. Bolan had told her of the route he had planned, as far as the Romanian frontier. It could have done as well for Albania as for Yugoslavia. But he had said nothing of the Gypsies.

"Our main problem is tracks," he said. "I guess the blizzard covered us when we lit out for the trees this morning. Otherwise they'd have been beating these woods like hunters after game. But any marks we leave now are going to stay there like signposts until it snows again."

"When will that be?"

He looked at the sky. "Not before night, I guess."

"Do we have to stay here until after dark then?"

Bolan shook his head. "Not right here. The longer we wait the more dangerous it will become. I think we should start right away."

"But—" she looked bewildered "—you just said. . . .''

"That we mustn't leave tracks, yeah. But look over there." He pointed to a depression about a quarter of a mile away, where a stream running into the valley had carved itself a shallow bed. The course of the stream was marked by a thicket of osiers. "Get in there, it'll take us down to the highway without anyone seeing us," Bolan said.

"But wouldn't we be blocked when we got there?" Ingrid objected. "I mean, there's a bridge across the river, but we'd hit the highway a good distance away from it. Walking along the road, we'd be worse off than we are here, surely?"

"Who needs bridges?" Bolan said.

He pointed again. On the far side of the road, the river ran between lines of poplar and alder trees. Through branches sparkling with frost she could see the surface, pearl gray and shining in the splintered sunlight. "Who needs bridges," Bolan repeated, "when the river's frozen and we can walk across? Or skate if we can find some kids to rob!"

She smiled and rose to her feet. "Let us go," she said.

The depression was called a cirque—steep sided, stony, sinuous and packed densely with young trees. It was tough going. The osiers whipped their faces and tangled with the Kalashnikovs. The snow beneath was patchy but there was enough of it to mask the roughness of the rocky, treacherous incline. The rivulet and its cascades were frozen solid. Bolan's ankle no longer pained him but he had to be extra careful not to wrench it again.

It was more than an hour later when they finally arrived, breathless and scratched, at the culvert that led the stream beneath the roadway. The sun, low in the western sky, had withdrawn behind a menacing cloud bank. The light was fading and it was colder than ever.

Bolan parted the branches and looked up and down the road.

Since midday there had been a fair bit of traffic. The snow was hard-packed with the marks of tires, chains, caterpillars and an occasional deep rut scored by an iron-rimmed cart wheel frozen into it. Away to the right, bare trees half concealed the white roofs of a village on the far side of the Dnieper. The bridge was three hundred yards in the other direction. Five arches spanned the wide sweep of the river.

At the near end, half a dozen soldiers were posted around a parked Zil 4x4 truck.

There was a rattle of chains from the direction of the village. Bolan and the woman crouched at the entrance to the culvert. An army command car with a fishing-rod antenna raced past, showering them with chips of ice. It stopped next to the bridge. Bolan could see an officer beside the driver pointing up toward the trees. He looked over his shoulder.

In the distance, high up against the valley slope, he saw a long line of men combing the edge of the wood. Faintly he could hear the deep-throated barking of dogs.

"Searching for tracks or trying to flush us," Bolan murmured. "Whatever, those animals are going find some trace, somewhere. We'd better go."

Ingrid stared at him. "Yes, but. . . ."

He nodded toward the mouth of the culvert.

It was a concrete pipe perhaps thirty inches in diameter. Dead branches, leaves, twigs and other fragments of rubbish swept down by the stream had become immured in the trickle of water frozen along the base of the culvert, but daylight was visible at the far end. Bolan figured it was the best way to crawl to the far side of the highway unseen.

"Won't do a lot of good to your coat," Bolan said, indicating Ingrid's gray astrakhan, already stiff and spiked from the blizzard. "You better get out of it, bundle it up and shove it along ahead of you."

"The coat is the least of my worries," Ingrid replied. But she took it off just the same.

The crossing was not difficult but it seemed endless. Twice the ground shook and a heavy rumbling assailed their ears as a convoy of some sort passed overhead. They could hear too, louder now, the approaching sounds of the dogs. But at last Bolan and the woman extricated themselves at the top of a cut that ran straight down to the riverbank.

Ingrid shrugged back into the coat and they ran bent double behind the alders for the bridge. It was almost dusk and a white mist was rising on the far side of the river.

The baying of the dogs rose to a triumphant climax. "They must have found the scent, probably where we were waiting up there," Bolan muttered. "Let's hope the cirque will fool them for a while."

"How could they have found the scent?"

"We left the grenade launcher under the brambles," he reminded her. "Both of us handled it, remember?"

The guards at the bridge were chattering excitedly, their attention on the trackers spread out over the hillside above. Bolan and the woman stepped onto the frozen surface of the river.

From arch to arch they slid cautiously over the black ice, flattening themselves against the brickwork as they passed to the outside of each pier.

No guards blocked the far end of the bridge and the fugitives were able to scramble up the bank and make the road, which plunged between steep banks and then turned right in the direction of the village.

"The coat may be the least of your worries," Bolan said when they felt safe enough to walk upright again, "but it heads the list of mine. We have to change clothes and quit this area fast. Our descriptions will have been broadcast countrywide."

A quarter of a mile from the bridge a load of granite chips for resurfacing the roadway had been dumped in a widened area hollowed from the bank. Leaning against the snow-covered heap were two bicycles.

Bolan stopped.

He looked up and down the lane.

There had been less traffic this side of the river. The snow had not yet been compacted. The tracks were clear. The bicycles had come from the village, and—

"That's odd," Bolan exclaimed.

"What is it?"

"The tracks." He pointed to the tire marks. From each machine a single line of footprints led to a rectangle about fifteen feet by five feet where the snow had scarcely covered the ground.

There were no other footprints.

"There must have been a car waiting here for some time," Bolan said, indicating the rectangle. "Obviously it was a rendezvous. Only one set of footprints, see. The riders must have arrived here, dismounted, walked to the car...."

"And then?"

"They must have got into the car and been driven away, leaving their bikes here. There's no other explanation that fits those footmarks. And there aren't any more—" he walked a few yards in each direction, scrutinizing the ground "—none at all anywhere around this turnout."

"So what do we do?"

"We take the bikes," Bolan said.

"Suppose the owners plan to come back and collect them later?"

"Well, that would be just too bad. But I don't think they intend to. You don't leave bikes out in the open, no chains locking the wheels, if you want to find them when you come back. Not in a country where you dare not even leave the blades on your windshield wipers."

"Very well. Which way do we ride?"

"According to the map, there should be a dirt road

leading up to the ridge on this side of the river. It's a left turn just before the village. We'll take that.''

Bolan strode across to the bicycles and hauled them upright. ''The sooner the better,'' he said. ''A guy dressed like me and a woman in astrakhan, both biking with Kalashnikovs slung across their backs, could cause a certain amount of comment right now, especially in these parts. But we won't ride for long,'' he added. ''We have to find a change of clothes and food, even if we have to do it at gunpoint.''

They were a hundred yards from the intersection, pedaling sedately side by side, when two militiamen stepped out from the side road and shouted at them to stop.

It was evident that the Russians had already recognized them from descriptions furnished by their superiors, because the moment Bolan yelled, ''The ditch! Quick!'' and vaulted from the saddle to the roadside, the two men opened fire.

What was equally clear was that the duo were both overeager and inexperienced, otherwise they would have waited until the cyclists had advanced to a more vulnerable position.

The error cost them their lives.

Bolan flung himself flat in a depression beneath the hedge that bordered the road, the Kalashnikov unslung before he hit the ground. Ingrid was already prone in the snow on the other side.

Slugs plowed into the drifts or whined over their heads. Bolan sighted the AK-74 as the militiamen stopped firing and ran for the intersection. It took a long burst that exhausted the magazine to bring one of them down. He rolled to the roadside, twitched, then lay still.

Bolan slammed in the spare.

Ingrid was shooting at a holly bush on the corner, behind which the other man was lurking. Eventually he darted out to take a shot at her. Bolan was ready. He ripped off a volley.

The militiaman fell to one knee, picked himself up and lurched to the center of the road, firing again from the hip.

Another burst from Bolan. The guy went down, rolled over, staggered upright and zigzagged back toward the intersection.

This time Bolan's shots were dead on target. The Russian was hurled backward into the holly bush. He slid to the ground, snow shaken from the leaves by the impact covering him like a shroud.

They recovered the bicycles and took the track uphill.

This time they left the AKs behind, since both weapons were now empty.

The wind was freshening. From across the river the baying of the dogs swelled and then faded. Helicopters with searchlights were skimming the treetops on the other side.

A vehicle with wide tires had made the hill. Keeping to its tracks, Bolan and Ingrid managed to stay in the saddle for all but the last hundred yards before the crest.

After that it was a downhill ride through the twilight until the trail again rose, more steeply this time. Breathless, they dismounted and began for the second time to push the machines.

A Lada station wagon was parked in front of a gate at the entrance to a farm track. Snow coated the hood and lay inches thick on the roof, the rear window and front windshield. In the gathering dusk the vehicle appeared to be empty but the keys were in the ignition.

"This is too good to be true," Bolan said. He stared over the gate. He saw a wooden farmhouse with a light showing in one window, but it was half hidden behind a swell of land that glimmered palely in the near dark.

They left the bikes and took the station wagon.

Beyond the next ridge, Bolan figured it would be safe to turn on the lights.

He was reaching for the ignition when he felt a ring of cold metal pressed to the back of his head.

16

"We're taking the woman," an American-accented voice drawled behind Bolan's ear. "You keep on driving."

The best method of defense is attack. How many times had Mack Bolan heard that in infantry training? How many times had he followed the advice in his one-man crusade against the slimebucket elements that threatened to corrupt the world? Against the Cong in Nam, against the mob, against the KGB, even against the pen-pushing bureaucrats who stifled progress in his own country? If Bolan had a fighting credo, that was it.

But for this one time, with a gun barrel pressed hard against the back of his head, he was going to turn away from his belief.

In the rear-view mirror Bolan could see two figures crowding the back seat.

He had no idea who the hijackers were. He could not make out their features in the dark.

They said they were taking the woman. They probably knew she was valuable.

And Bolan was certain that the Lada station wagon had been left there specifically to trap him. He berated himself for not properly checking the interior of the vehicle in the growing darkness. But even as he did so he realized that the desire to get himself and the woman back across the border far outweighed the risks inherent in their present situation.

But how had his captors known he would be coming this way? He had no idea.

They had the drop on him. The second man had already reached forward and lifted the Tokarev from his pocket.

Bolan knew that any overt action on his part would result either in his death, his disablement or at best his being thrown out of the car.

But he figured he stood a fair chance of getting away.

Then he'd be a free agent. He would be able to follow them, attack at a moment of his choice when *he* had the drop on *them*, and get Ingrid away from them.

Yeah. According to the map, which he hoped they had not studied sufficiently, the road petered out ten miles farther on, after which there were only footpaths and forest rides crossing the highlands to Tarashcha. From there secondary roads led the remaining fifty-five miles to Vinnitsa, but Bolan figured on catching up well before then.

After that he'd have to play it by ear. For now the important thing was to duck out.

There was no opportunity for him to warn Ingrid. He noticed that the door handle would open downward. The muzzle of the gun was no longer touching his head. Time to move.

Bolan erupted into action. He hit the handle, shoving the door outward with all his strength, and dived in one fluid movement as the car negotiated a sharp right-hand bend in the trail.

A hot wind of flame scorched the top of his head as he pitched forward. He heard the shot, the crash of exploding glass from the window and a shout of alarm all at the same time.

Rutted snow and the hard earth beneath it leaped upward to clobber him as the car lurched away.

Bolan shoulder-rolled, came up kneeling, saw the taillights of the Lada swing crazily from side to side, straighten up and then blaze brightly as the car came to a halt. He figured that one of the men must have seized the wheel to keep them on the road and then slid over into the driver's seat and braked.

Bolan was hoping they'd get out to look for him. It would be one on one, because they wouldn't leave Ingrid alone. In the dark in thick woods, Bolan unarmed would back himself against any one man with a handgun.

The attackers must have been thinking along the same lines, because after a moment, the engine revved and the Lada jerked into motion again.

Bolan was already concealed in the brushwood. As soon as he saw that the car was really on its way, not just making a sham start to tempt him into the open, he went back to the road and started walking.

The trees grew more closely as the road rose. Stars shone brightly in the channel of sky visible above it. The night air was bitter, freezing Bolan's fingers and stinging his face from time to time with tiny particles of ice. Once the sound of the Lada's engine had faded and died it was very quiet. The moan of the wind somewhere above him was punctuated only by the soft thump of falling snow as a branch shook free its burden, and the crunching of his footsteps on the rutted roadway.

He had been walking for twenty minutes when he heard the noise of a laboring engine. This time it came from behind. Soon the long beams of headlights bounced across the snow, flinging a shadow in front of the striding man.

Bolan listened carefully. One vehicle. It didn't sound like a military unit. But he'd take no chances. He left the road and headed for the undergrowth.

The vehicle was going very slowly. Too slowly. The lights brightened, became blinding. Stopped moving when they were level with his hiding place. "You wish a ride?" a voice called out of the dark.

Bolan said nothing.

"You don't have to be frightened," the voice said. The accent was foreign but the words were Russian. "I have nothing to do with the authorities, the KGB or the militia."

Still Bolan remained silent, frowning. Was this bone-chilling cold playing tricks on him? There was something in that voice.... No, this was the middle of nowhere.

"Come on out." A little impatient now. "I know you're there. I have been following your tracks. They lead right in to where you are. I know you are unarmed too."

Bolan shrugged. He walked warily back to the road, keeping well behind the headlight beams.

It was a pickup truck, sand-colored or yellow, judging from the curve of bodywork reflected by the lights. There appeared to be only one man in it. "It's too cold a night to be walking," he said. "I thought you would like a ride."

What the hell! "Maybe I would," Bolan said. He skirted the rear of the vehicle and climbed into the passenger seat. "Thanks, pal."

The driver shoved the lever into first and they moved off. "Going far?" he asked when they had traveled a few hundred yards.

"Right to the end of the line," Bolan said.

"Me too," said the driver. "The end of the line."

Something in the tone of his voice made Bolan turn sharply and stare.

Bolan caught his breath. His stare became more intent. In the dim greenish light cast upward from the dashboard he saw that he was riding with the thin man who had come to their aid during the fight with the militiamen in the bus outside the factory.

17

The dogs traced the fugitives to the culvert before dark, then along the embankment to the bridge. Once on the far side it was a simple matter of deduction from the fresh tracks in the snow—the bicycles, the two dead militiamen at the intersection, the route leading to the farm. The floodlights of Strakhov's helicopter had swept over the gate and the farm track within ten minutes of the discovery of the abandoned bikes.

The major who had been in command of the detail at the bridge stepped down from the reconnaissance car and saluted as Strakhov jumped from the grounded chopper's open hatch.

"It seems, comrade General," he said, "that the assassins had an accomplice waiting here with a car. It is to be assumed that there were others. Somebody must have left those bicycles for them."

"A car was also waiting there," Strakhov said shortly. "Or so I have been told. But there are too many footmarks to determine what happened. Do you not think it strange, however, that the escape should be split between bicycles and a car when the turnout and this farm are so close? Why not make the rendezvous with the car? Why use bicycles at all? And why park again here?"

Kopalsky, the militia chief, had been examining the tracks around the gate. "It is clear, comrade General," he said, "that there were indeed more than two persons involved here. Apart from the footprints made by the

American and the woman traitor, there are two if not three other sets visible. It would be my guess that all of them left in the vehicle. All, that is, except...." He looked hesitantly at the major.

"Except what?" Strakhov demanded.

The major shifted his feet in the snow. "There was...one individual," he said, "who did not leave in the car."

Strakhov was fuming. "I thought we were dealing with a single renegade American and a woman who might or might not be a traitor. Don't tell me we have a conspiracy on our hands?" He stared at the major. "You said 'was'?"

The officer looked uncomfortable. "We saw a light in the farmhouse when we arrived, comrade General. We surrounded the building as quickly and as quietly as possible. The light was extinguished and the person inside attempted to evade my men. They caught him, but before he could be questioned, he...I am afraid he was in possession of some kind of death pill...cyanide, I imagine...and, well, unfortunately we were too late."

"Felicitations," Strakhov said sarcastically. "The one witness we have to this catalog of inefficiency, and you let him—"

He broke off as a militiaman, slipping on the frozen snow, ran up to them from the lane. "With respect, comrade General," he said breathlessly, "the tracks show that a second vehicle has been driven toward the ridge."

"Then we will follow," Strakhov decided. "The road ends in ten miles. Both cars will have to be abandoned there and the occupants, if they are connected, must continue on foot. If we throw a wide enough cordon around that area we should have them in the net before morning."

"There will be some difficulty, sir, completing the circle in time," the major said dubiously. "The half-tracks can only go as far as the road. The trees are very dense there. And it is a huge detour over rough country, to approach from the far side. I don't—"

"In helicopters, imbecile," Strakhov snapped. "We shall pursue them as far as the end of the road in this." He gestured toward the BRDM-2. "And then your men can follow their tracks on foot and radio approximate positions to the pilots."

With a spotlight trained on the roadway, the scout car took the general, together with Kopalsky, the major and his men, in the direction of the ridge. Colonel Antonin remained with Zhukov, the MVD official, in the helicopter. They were to return to the army air base at Sumy and organize the troop carriers that would ferry soldiers to the area.

When the scout car's spotlight showed up the confusion of tracks where Bolan had left the road, then accepted a ride in the pickup, the officers got out to examine the marks in the snow.

But the clues there and at the farm were not sufficiently explicit, even for the most skillful among them, to deduce the sequence of events before their arrival.

"The truth can wait. We shall force it out of them when they're in the bag," Strakhov growled. "Right now the important thing is to lay our hands on that bastard Bolan." He climbed back into the scout car. "The end of the road, and make it quick," he told the driver.

FRANK SANTAYANA AND PHILIPPE PELLER had prepared their getaway well. Far from ignoring the fact that the road petered out on the edge of a forest, they had already taken it into account and turned it to their advantage. Two hundred yards along the footpath that succeeded the road, they had found a woodcutters' hut in a small clearing, and there, two days before, they had hidden a motorcycle combination, which was narrow enough and maneuverable enough to be threaded between the closely packed trees where no four-wheeled vehicle could penetrate.

The bike was a BMW with a torpedo-shaped aluminum sidecar.

Before they abandoned the Lada station wagon, Ingrid Korsun had been gagged with strips of tape and forced at gunpoint to walk to the hut. Now her wrists and ankles were bound and she was laid flat in the sidecar, from which the seat had been removed, with her head toward the bulbous front and her feet in the pointed tail.

Santayana clipped a canvas cover over the cockpit as though the sidecar was unoccupied, and climbed onto the pillion seat behind Peller. For three hours they corkscrewed through the forest, sometimes following the footpath, sometimes making a shortcut between the trees.

In the Lada, the two CIA agents had spoken very little, because they did not want their captive to know who or what they were. The woman had said nothing, remained icily contemptuous and aloof. Riding the motorcycle, the two men were even less talkative.

The three hours of low-gear travel brought them no more than twenty-five miles closer to the farther edge of the forest. And by then the freshening wind had blown over more snow from the east.

Large flakes drifted down between the laced branches of the trees and whirled toward the riders in the light carved by the BMW's headlamp. They had breasted the final ridge and were dropping down in the direction of the open country beyond, when Peller left the trail and headed for the CIA's second safe house in the region.

It was a wooden hunting lodge, a summer holiday home for embassy personnel. Peller ran the combination in under the steep roof of an outhouse and cut the engine. "I hope Emil shows soon on the other BMW," the woman heard him say.

"Yeah, what about that guy?" Santayana said. "Who is he?"

"A sleeper for years. He works as a lecturer at the Kiev technical college. I hated to leave him at the farm like that, but—"

"You're gonna have to wait," Santayana interrupted, "whether he shows or not. It's blowing up a storm out there. My guess is that we'll have blizzard conditions again within the hour."

MACK BOLAN was twenty feet up in the branches of a silver birch when Strakhov's trackers hurried past on the trail of the combination. The men were now wearing snow fatigues, white one-piece coveralls equipped with a hood, over their uniforms. There were six of them, spread out in a rough zigzag formation over a seventy-yard front.

Bolan waited until they were some way off and then swarmed back to the ground. Moving as silently as a wraith, he flitted between the trees, following the bobbing flashlights of the search party. Some distance behind he could hear other voices muffled by the snow, but when he looked back there was nothing to see.

The thin man who had twice come to his rescue had set him down near the end of the road and had driven the pickup off toward what looked like a small shack some time before. Bolan was no nearer solving the mystery of his identity, of his appearances and disappearances, of the reasons behind his actions, than he had been when the guy first leaped into the fray during the bus battle.

Throughout the ten-mile ride, the thin man had remained noncommittal, parrying Bolan's questions and continuing to refer to himself simply as "a friend in need." If he in turn knew anything of Bolan or his mission he kept it to himself.

As Bolan climbed out of the pickup, its driver had come across with a parting gift. "You may need this," he said. "The tracks will show up better with a little illumination." And he handed Bolan a flashlight.

Goddamn! How the hell had he known Bolan was tracking?

The light beam was essential just the same. Without it Bolan would never have seen the motorcycle tire marks spiraling between the trees.

He was about a mile along the forest path when he heard the approach of the soldiers and shinned up the birch.

His mind seethed with the complexity of the problems facing him. Who were the two guys that kidnapped Ingrid? Their voices sounded American. Did that mean that Fort Meade and Langley had got wind of the RIAMS computer and were making a play for it themselves? Yes or no, he had to find them, best them and get her back, fast.

The numbers were running out. They weren't so far from the frontier and he had yet to explain to her his own deceit. In addition to that, the Russians were uncomfortably close. Until he could get Ingrid clear of the immediate area, he could not let up, dared not relax long enough to establish some kind of personal relationship.

Also, the greatest problem still remained, a task that had haunted him since the first few hours of the mission: the "conversion" of the woman.

If he was going to deal successfully with all of these problems—and Bolan never lost confidence in his own ability to live large—there was no time to waste. The action had to start—like now.

The arrival of the soldiers provided the opportunity he needed, the chance to keep up with them and at the same time keep clear of them. He would take, as he always did, a gamble.

Shadowing them through the forest, he moved progressively out toward the man on the right flank. He was the one who was farthest away from his neighbor.

Bolan's opportunity came when the soldier's path led him into a slight hollow surrounded by bushes.

The man was bent over, searching the light snow cover for tracks, his flashlight swinging right and left. Bolan padded swiftly to the lip of the depression... and jumped.

Everything depended on a silent attack. His heels crashed savagely against the Russian's shoulders, flattening him to the frozen ground, knocking the breath from his lungs and extinguishing his flashlight.

Bolan's steely hand closed in a viselike grip over the fallen man's mouth and nose, stifling any cry. The Executioner knelt on the small of his back, groping for the windpipe with his free hand.

The fingers began to squeeze. His thumb located the vulnerable point uniting artery and nerve.

And pressed.

The guy threshed from side to side, trying to throw Bolan off. His arms flailed despairingly, scuffing up powdered snow. Bolan increased the pressure. The soldier spent all his tomorrows in a last convulsion, and then went limp.

Bolan was stripping off the white snow fatigues when the NCO in charge of the detail called: "Bulianov? Where are you, man? What happened?"

Bolan had heard enough of the dead man's voice calling out to the others when traces of the motorcycle combination were visible, to manage a passable imitation. "Fell," he replied gruffly. "Damned tree root."

"Well, look sharp and catch up. We don't want any lost ground."

Pulling on the coveralls, Bolan grunted something unintelligible. Bulianov had carried a holstered service revolver on his hip. Bolan stuffed the gun in his pocket. He picked up the Kalashnikov, switched on his own flashlight and hurried after the others.

Fortunately most of the tracks in that part of the forest were on the detail's left flank. Half an hour passed before "Bulianov" was called upon to speak again.

This time Bolan was not so lucky. The combination had veered away from the footpath and taken a wide sweep in his direction. The man on his left yelled a question that Bolan failed to understand. He made a noncommittal reply, but the Russian became suspicious. He strode toward Bolan, his voice rising querulously.

In white snow fatigues against a snow-covered background in torchlight, Bolan might pass despite his height for one of the soldiers. But in close-up it was something else. He allowed the man to come within striking distance and, while his mouth was still open with astonishment at the sight of a stranger, felled him with a single powerful blow.

This time the NCO was not deceived. "What the hell is going on over there?" he cried, unslinging his assault rifle.

Bolan shoved his own onto full automatic and dropped to the ground. Propped on his elbows, lying prone, he prepared to fire.

STRAKHOV AND HIS TWO COMPANIONS heard the fusillade as they followed up along the forest pathway. "I believe they've got him at last!" the KGB chief cried exultantly. Half running, ahead of the other officers, he hurried toward the sound of the shots.

But there was no reply when he radioed the NCO.

The NCO was never going to reply again to anyone. He lay with four of his men where he had fallen, flakes of snow that had drifted from the branches above decorating his bloodied chest with posthumous medals of frozen pink.

Strakhov's rage was spectacular. He called his Swidnik and ordered the pilot to pick him up at the entrance to the forest. He instructed the base at Sumy to dispatch troop-carriers to the far side of the forest and deploy men who were to start searching for motorcycle tracks, penetrating from that end. Then, choking with fury, he stamped back toward the roadway and the waiting chopper.

MACK BOLAN DOGGEDLY FOLLOWED the tracks made by the combination. He had covered less than ten miles when it began to snow heavily. Soon even beneath the trees the tire marks were obliterated.

He continued along the footpath, guessing that the two Americans must have gone in the same general direction. With a prisoner to hide from the KGB, Bolan was sure they had a specific goal somewhere on the far side of the forested ridge.

He decided to continue until he caught up. It never occurred to him that he might lose them. In any case, there was nothing else he could do. To retreat now would be unthinkable.

By the time the full force of the blizzard was unleashed, the batteries of his flashlight were almost exhausted. Finally the light died on him altogether. He struggled on indomitably through the white hell of the storm. Once or twice over the howl of the wind he thought he heard the sound of helicopters, but for the most part he was battling the elements as though he was the only man left alive. The whirling squalls plastered icy flakes against his mouth and nose, blinding his eyes, soaking and then freezing the coverall and the clothes beneath.

Crucified by fatigue, a terrible hunger gnawing his belly, he lost all sense of time, keeping his direction purely by instinct as he fought his way a yard at a time through the deepening snow.

Only a man of Bolan's iron will could have persevered in such conditions. Throughout the hours of darkness and on into the bitter cold of the day that followed, his numbed limbs kept moving.

It was not until noon that his hellish trek ended. As he staggered exhausted from the forest, the blizzard at last blew itself out and a fugitive patch of blue appeared between the scudding clouds.

Half a mile away across a waist-deep snowfield he saw the hunting lodge.

And behind a line of skeletal trees, a snowplow followed by two six-wheeled Ural-375 army trucks full of soldiers moved slowly up a lane that led from the building to the valley below.

A few minutes later the rumble of their laboring engines was drowned by the whir of rotors as two helicopters flew in from the east and hovered above the lodge.

18

"Do we start shooting or do we split?" Frank Santayana asked. "The bastards are surrounding the place, but we could still make it through that thicket behind the outhouse."

"We stay and fight," Peller told him. "We'd never get clear with the woman. Not through all that. I mean she's not exactly a willing accomplice, is she? But we should have a good chance if we can write off this first wave here, before the big stuff shows. We have the cover. They're out in the open, perfect targets against the snow."

"Just as you say," Santayana replied. "You're the director."

But the two CIA men found that the soldiers were not such perfect targets when they had donned white snow fatigues and moved away from their transports. There were about two dozen of them, armed with assault rifles, grenades and submachine guns.

"As long as we stop them before they reach the trees," Peller said, "we should be okay. They'll have RPG-7s but I don't think they'll use them because of the girl. We have to try and keep them from lobbing in gas grenades."

"Those guys are not militia, are they? Hell, I didn't bargain on a fight with the Red Army."

"Army or not, they'll be controlled by the KGB, or the KGB in association with the GRU. This character Strakhov has pull. If it bugs you shooting down honest Russians, think of the scenario if we're caught."

"I know," Santayana said. "The Lubyanka and then the labor camps."

"So start shooting," said Peller.

Beneath the floorboards of the safe house, there had been half a dozen assault rifles, a box of antipersonnel stick grenades and two gas-operated M-60 machine guns with tripods. The rifles were now stacked against the inner wall, and the M-60s had been mounted to fire out of windows facing east and south as soon as Peller had seen the snowplow.

Each of the machine guns was provided with two link belts of 7.62mm ammunition and there were spare 5.56mm magazines for the rifles. The woman, still bound and gagged, was in a room upstairs.

Santayana fired a burst at the men disembarking from the trucks while Peller hosed the advance guard hurrying through the snow toward the shelter of the trees behind the lodge.

The noise was deafening. Spent shell cases fountained from the breeches of the machine guns. Blue smoke hazed the wood-walled room.

Out in the snow, men staggered, spun and fell. Half a dozen had been zapped before return fire spewed from the trucks. Then soldiers hidden between the two helicopters and a line of bushes bordering the lane started shooting. Wood splintered from the window embrasures as the hail of lead hammered the walls of the lodge.

There was a depression in the snowfield between the building and the lane, a dip in the land that was indistinguishable against the blinding white cover but all too obvious when men crouching low half vanished and then disappeared entirely behind it.

"Goddamn," Santayana panted. "I never realized they'd catch up so soon. I thought we might have to deal with Bolan again, but.... Where do you suppose the guy is, anyway?"

"You tell me." Peller shrugged, reaching for the second link belt. "Back where he jumped, I guess. He's unarmed, he's got no transport, he can't do no harm."

Beside the Ural trucks someone was shouting orders. The giant snowplow moved slowly toward the lodge, its great scoop held out in front like a shield. Behind it, a line of soldiers advanced grimly.

"Make them keep their heads down," Peller yelled. "I've got to open fire from the back and stop the comrades making those trees."

He grabbed one of the rifles, hefted his M-60 and dashed through to the kitchen. The soldiers hidden in the hollow were just emerging to race for the thicket. Peller opened fire again.

But there were four walls to the lodge and only two men to defend them. Inexorably, despite their casualties, the Russians closed in.

Peller panned the M-60 from side to side as far as the window would allow. Santayana exhausted his second belt and the hard chatter of the machine gun was replaced by whip-crack shots from one of the rifles.

More soldiers fell. But the rate of fire from outside increased as the range grew shorter.

Finally it was Peller who ducked out, escaping behind a log pile and then tunneling through the snow to the thicket and the forest beyond.

Santayana stayed in the front room of the lodge. He had thrown one stick grenade that fell short and was standing up behind the machine gun to hurl another, when a marksman behind the snowplow drilled him between the eyes with a single shot. The grenade exploded just outside the window, wrecking the room. Santayana was slammed back against the wall by the blast. He slumped to the floor, bringing down the remaining rifles to form a triumphal arch over his lifeless body.

"Mexican?" Strakhov snarled ten minutes later,

looking at the dead man's ID papers. "A trade delegate? This is an American Embassy building. Believe me, there will be some expulsions from Moscow after this. We have an opportunity to rid ourselves of certain diplomatic undesirables here!"

"But do you think, comrade General," Antonin ventured, "that the abduction was a CIA plot? Is the man Bolan connected with that organization?"

"I do not know what to think." For once Strakhov was at a loss. "I expected to find Bolan here, to trap him here—but the description of the criminal who got away does not fit. It does not fit at all." He shook his head. "In any case, according to my information, our plan to discredit Bolan was one hundred percent successful. The CIA even had a contract out on him at one time."

"So you think, comrade General, that Bolan was not here at all?"

"We shall see. The woman should have some information on that point. Among—" the voice suddenly menacing "—many others."

Ingrid Korsun was brought down to ground floor level. She was still tied to a chair from which long slivers of wood had been gouged by the attackers' bullets. The astrakhan coat was in rags. One sleeve was half torn from the shoulder. Her face was dirty.

Colonel Antonin moved to tear off the crisscross of tape gagging her mouth, but Strakhov held up a restraining hand. "Leave her. I want her first words officially recorded. It will be more convenient to transport her to Kiev like this. In such a condition you should have no trouble with her."

Between the mussed hair and the gag, the woman's blue eyes blazed furiously at the KGB chief. He smiled. "I must return there myself at once. We will deal with Bolan later. In the meantime a team of expert inter-

rogators have to be briefed. We must make sure this dis-
loyal bitch spills everything she knows. Everything.''

"Do you wish me—'' Antonin began.

"I shall leave now in the first helicopter. You will
follow with the prisoner in the second machine. The
army can clear up this mess here and report to you later
through the GRU." Strakhov nodded once and left the
room.

Two soldiers carried the squirming body of Ingrid
Korsun to the remaining Swidnik. She was stowed un-
ceremoniously behind the seats in the blister. The pilot
had already fired up the turboshafts and was sitting with
his right hand on the throttle.

Antonin stared at the helmeted and goggled figure.
The pilot was swathed in a fleece-lined leather topcoat.
"What are you playing at?" the colonel demanded. "It
may be winter but this is a heated cabin. Why are you
dressed in that absurd fashion?"

"So that you don't recognize me too soon," Mack
Bolan said.

He swung around fast, the service revolver he had
taken from Bulianov in his left hand. The gun barked
once.

Antonin fell backward through the open hatch,
spraying the snow with scarlet. The slug had torn
through his left shoulder only inches from the heart.

The helicopter soared into the air, canted over and
whirled away toward the south as the soldiers ran up
and opened fire.

19

The Swidnik skimmed across the valley, rose above the swell of land on the far side and headed for the Carpathian foothills. "I figure on ten minutes, no more, before we have to put down and run," Bolan told Ingrid Korsun. Five of those minutes had already passed by the time he leaned over the back of his seat and cut her free.

"Why so soon?" the woman asked, rubbing her wrists to restore the circulation. She scrambled across and lowered herself into the seat beside him.

"MiGs," Bolan said briefly. "Give them a few minutes to recover from the loss of one chopper and one colonel, a little more time to get to the radio, then it'll be a flight of chase planes scrambled from Sumy. It'll only take them six or seven minutes to get here, using afterburners."

"Will they find it so easy to see us?" She stared down through the blister at the wooded country below. "Against all those trees?"

"We're not in the ADIZ yet—" Bolan began.

"The what?"

"Air defense identification zone. Near the frontier. Where unexpected, unidentified aircraft have a last chance to explain themselves. Inland from there it's seek and destroy. We are below the radar defenses, but any of those fighter jets passing within five miles of us, we show up as a blip on their individual screens."

Like the waves of a fossilized sea, the snow-covered

land below rolled in a series of alternating crests and troughs toward a coastline of distant mountains.

"We need to make it somewhere near a small town," Bolan said.

"But isn't that dangerous?"

"Safer than in open country where every stranger is a landmark. Do you still have the money?"

"Yes."

"Good. Let's look for a small town. We'll be able to buy different clothes and something to eat. Then we can find an inn or a hotel and hole up for one or two days."

"Would it not be safer in a city? To be lost in a crowd?"

Bolan shook his head. "A small town," he repeated, "big enough for two foreigners not to attract too much attention but small enough not to be ready and organized for immediate roadblocks or military patrols. Too many authorities in a city." He paused and then added, "In any case, we're not within fifty miles of any city." He pointed ahead through the Plexiglas. "Here they come!"

Three dartlike shadows streaked across the sky a couple of miles ahead of them.

"MiG-28s," Bolan said. "Let's hope they don't have heat-seeking missiles aboard. Hold on, we're going down."

The chopper plummeted toward the trees.

"It takes them fifteen miles to make a 180-degree turn," Bolan said. "That's the one chance we've got."

Bolan knew they'd been sighted on the chase planes' radar screens. The three MiGs made a pass, the thunder of their motors drowning the Swidnik's own jet-whine. The helicopter rocked in the hot turbulence of their passage. Bright streaks of flame arced ahead of them and dropped into the forest.

"Rockets. They're not radio directed," Bolan said.

He sideslipped the chopper giddily, dropping toward a clearing between the trees. Three miles away, the snow-covered roofs of a small town clustered around a bell tower at the head of a valley. A bridge carried railroad tracks over an iced-up river to a yard where factory chimneys pointed black fingers at the sky.

The helicopter slammed down into the clearing and bounced on its skids. Bolan had the hatch open while the rotors were still raising swirls of snow from the ground. "Quick!" he yelled. "Into the trees on the far side. And get down, fast."

There was a rushing roar. An express train screech. In arrowhead formation the three fighters flashed momentarily into sight above the trees.

Bolan grabbed the rifle he had taken from Bulianov and leaped after the girl, flinging himself down on a bed of frozen pine needles when he heard the jets making their second approach.

This time they came in line ahead. Rockets hissed down into the clearing, scattering snow, plowing up the earth beneath, setting the damp buried grass ablaze, bursting with a series of sharp ripping detonations that sounded like a sheet of calico tearing, magnified a hundred times. At least three of them made direct hits on the Swidnik.

The chopper erupted. For a microsecond, imprinted on the dark background of the woods, it stood limned in fire. And then as the fuel tanks exploded, the whole machine ballooned into a scorching fireball that marbled with crimson the black smoke cloud bellying skyward.

One of the MiGs made a final run, presumably to check out results and photograph the damage, then they reformed and flew away to the north.

Bolan raised his head. There was no sound in the glade but the crackle of flaming pines set alight by the explosion. Fragments of the helicopter lay strewed over the smoking grass and the skeleton of its fuselage and stub wings still burned fiercely. One of the rotor blades was jammed into the fork of a tree.

"Okay," Bolan said tightly. "While they think that was our funeral pyre and before they send the meat wagon to recover our corpses, let's get out of here and go find something to eat."

He stripped off the fleece-lined coat and gave it to the woman—she had left the ruined astrakhan in the helicopter—then, picking up the rifle, he led the way downhill through the trees.

"YOU ARE VERY BRAVE and you are strong," Ingrid Korsun said. "More than that, you persevere. To a scientist perseverance, the will to follow something through to the end, is perhaps the most valuable quality of all."

"I do what has to be done," Bolan said simply.

They were in a hotel room overlooking a river. The town was called Pervomaysk. It was about one hundred miles from the Romanian frontier. The river was the Sinyukha. It ran southeast toward Odessa and the Black Sea, where the estuary lay between the Dnieper and the Dniester.

There had been no trouble getting there. Shopping separately, they had bought clothes, beer and sausage, a small suitcase. Bolan had buried the rifle in a deserted sand pit on the outskirts of town and reverted to his East German identity. Ingrid pretended she was an Intourist woman showing him some less-known factories.

"Until I got to the lodge," Bolan said, "I had no idea it was Strakhov leading the hunt. We are old enemies. But it's okay, because when they find there are no bodies in the chopper, they will put out an all-stations alert. But it won't be for Herr Kurt Zimmermann, the electronics engineer from Leipzig. It will be for me, as myself. Also," he said grimly, "knowing that Strakhov's on the other side will give me an extra incentive to make damned sure that I succeed.''

Booking into the hotel had posed no problem either. It was a tall narrow building, six stories and no elevator, with a fire escape at the rear that led to a yard containing rows of trash cans and a rusted Trabant panel truck with four flats. The rooms at the rear, away from the noises of the street, were all taken but there were two adjoining rooms on the third floor front with a common balcony over the river.

Ingrid had occupied herself with the formalities. She had handed the gray, dispirited man behind the desk Bolan's German ID, Russian visa and trade fair pass. With them she had shown her own genuine identification. She was, to Bolan's astonishment, wearing an Intourist lapel badge. A girlfriend worked on the Intourist desk at the fair, she told Bolan later.

The man had copied down the details. The militia patrol making their routine check that evening would learn that an East German comrade was in town to study industrial techniques in use at the microchip research center and at the recycled-paper mill across the river. They would be unlikely to know of the defection of a female university professor from Kiev. If they did, or if the militia detail thought to check whether any visits to the factories had been organized... well, there was always the fire escape and the Kalashnikov in the sand pit.

They dined in a state restaurant across the street from the railroad station. Nobody paid any attention to them.

Throughout the evening Bolan became increasingly conscious of the enigmatic quality of Ingrid's character. She was evasive about her plans for living in China. She refused to talk about her political beliefs and she was cagey in her criticism of the Soviet regime. Even on the subject of electronics her enthusiasm was tempered with a certain reluctance. They were left with Russian literature, Russian movies and banalities concerning the climatic conditions in different Soviet states.

Bolan did not miss the aura of magnetic, almost feral, sensuality displayed by the big blonde with every move she made. He was agonizingly aware, sitting side by side in a narrow booth, of the proximity of her body to his own. He felt a tension building between them, unspoken and unacknowledged, at each sideways glance, each fleeting pressure of her thigh.

His own tenseness, the coiled-spring energy that always vibrated within him once the action started, was clamoring for release. By the time they finished the second vodka carafe and drained their cups of insipid coffee, his urge to touch her, caress her, seize her, take her, was overpowering.

They walked, studiously apart, by the frozen river. Pervomaysk was not exactly the last word in nightlife. In one *tavarna* a balalaika played; drunken voices sang in another. A cold wind blew tiny trails of snow along the cleared sidewalk.

Back in the hotel they stood facing one another outside Bolan's room at the top of the stairs. In the dim light from a low-powered electric lamp on the landing he could see the whites of her eyes. The central heating blew hot drafts through vents in the floor, Roman style.

Finally, Bolan bade Ingrid a gruff good-night and turned to unlock his door. He was aware of a stillness behind him. He turned around. She was standing motionless there, her arms straight down by her sides. "What are you doing?" he breathed.

"Waiting for you," she said simply.

He sensed the acceleration of his pulses. It was very close to the overheated stairwell. Suddenly it was also totally quiet, as though the world outside had stopped turning. He became conscious of their breathing, two of them, faster and faster.

He reached out and grasped the cool of her upper arms through the blue silk sleeves.

"There is something, is there not?" she whispered. "You feel it too. I know you do."

"You bet your sweet life I do," Bolan choked. He felt her shiver as his hands slid down to her elbows. "Your room or mine?"

"Mine," she said matter-of-factly. "It is more discreet. There is an outside wall at one side... and only you on the other."

The room had a rough pine floor, an Afghan rug beside a low iron bedstead, a faint odor of disinfectant and moonlight slanting through shutters. To Bolan and the woman, after the past two nights, it was oriental in its splendor.

Ingrid had unbuttoned her silk shirt and folded it neatly over a rail at one side of the marble-topped washstand. She was wearing a white brassiere and her full, firm breasts were straining against the confinement of the material. Bolan's throat went dry as he tore off his own clothes.

In the half-light, her body had an almost translucent quality, like bone china. She opened her lips slightly as Bolan moved toward her, moistening them with the tip of her tongue.

Bolan closed his mouth over hers, intoxicated through all his senses.

Slowly they sank to the bed and she locked her strong thighs around him....

He was awakened soon after six. Something in the character of the gray light filtering through the shutters, in the muffled quality of the early street noises below, told him that snow had fallen again during the night. Soon the alto whine of spinning wheels and the roar of revving engines confirmed the icy state of the roadway.

The woman beside Bolan stirred. Despite the heating, the dawn chill had penetrated the room. She drew the covers more tightly over her bare shoulder and snuggled closer to him. Beneath the weight of her breast, he could feel her heart beating strongly. A few inches from his face one of the blue eyes opened.

The eye widened. And then all at once he realized that her gaze was focused past him. He could feel his body going into combat mode.

Then, aware of movement behind him, and astonishment in the eyes before him, Bolan turned his head and saw what she had seen.

The thin man, the driver of the pickup. He was standing just inside the door and there was a Walther P5 in his hand.

"You...what the hell are you doing here?" Bolan shouted.

The stranger smiled his bird smile. "I see that this time you are in no need of a friend," he said. "But I am afraid this time I am an enemy in need."

"What are you talking about?" Bolan started to move away from the woman.

A brusque movement of the gun cut him short. "I do not have much time," the gunman said. "I have to leave here at once and I am taking comrade Korsun with me."

The irony of the moment did not escape the Executioner. He was caught with his pants down. The service revolver was in the pocket of his jacket on the floor beneath the window. "Who are you?" he demanded.

"The name is Kriplin," the intruder said. "Anton Kriplin, from Tirana in Albania."

20

Kriplin! The real Albanian. No wonder the guy had stuck around.

Bolan's forward planning collapsed like a house of cards. He stole a glance at Ingrid. How would she take the revelation that the man she had escaped with, the smartass who had talked her into risking her life, was an impostor? She was sitting on the far side of the bed with her back to him, pulling on her clothes.

"Why now?" Bolan came straight to the point. "Why didn't you make your play as soon as we left Kiev? Or even in the city itself?"

"I should have thought that was obvious." For the second time Kriplin's beaky features creased into a smile. "Once you were in the game it was smarter to let you run with the ball, and then take over, as I am doing now, not too long before the line. That way you take all the risks and I get the medal. The CIA operatives had the same idea."

"Had?"

"I think it's fair to use the past tense. They flunked out."

Ingrid had swung around when she heard the mention of the CIA. Now she moved across to the washstand and picked up her skirt, but she said nothing.

Bolan too was dressing. "So all the friend in need routine was a blind? You were keeping tabs, helping me to help yourself?"

"That's right. Now you're with it. But I'm not. The

one mystery left is you...Herr Zimmermann from
Leipzig. What are you doing here? Why should you
wish to make off with an electronics expert? Just who
are you working for—and why pass yourself off as
me?"

"Find out," the Executioner replied.

"I would if I had time," Kriplin agreed. "But I don't.
Arrangements for Comrade Korsun have already been
made. The flight plan east has been filed. Now that she
is at last with the right contact, I guess she'll be in a
hurry to get going?" He looked at the woman. She was
tidying the outer clothes Bolan had strewed on the floor
the night before, picking up his jacket from beneath the
window.

"That's right," she said.

Kriplin raised the gun. He took a perforated silencer
from his pocket and clicked it into position over the
Walther's barrel. "I am sorry about this," he told Bolan with genuine regret in his voice. "I really am. But
you must see that I have no choice. Knowing what you
know, I am sure you understand that I cannot afford to
leave you here alive. Not when we still have quite a way
to go. I will make it quick."

The long, holed tube lined up with Bolan's forehead.
Kriplin's forefinger flexed around the trigger.

The sound of the shot was deafening.

Smashed china shattered as the Albanian hurtled into
the night table and knocked a pitcher and basin to the
floor. Kriplin lay crumpled by the wall with half his face
blown away. Blood and brain tissue slid slowly down to
join him.

By the washstand, Ingrid Korsun stood trembling,
with Bolan's jacket still in her hands. The smoking barrel of the revolver she had fired projected through a hole
in the scorched pocket.

Bolan exploded into action. The questions could

come later. "Other side of the landing," he rasped. "The fire escape. Take the suitcase and anything else you can grab. But hurry, someone will be here in seconds."

He followed the woman from the room, still zipping up his pants. He had retained the fleece-lined coat; she had bought a *tchouba* lined with rabbit fur the previous day.

Already the hotel was echoing with voices. Bolan counted on initial shock—plus caution where firearms were concerned—to give them time to get clear. Heavy footsteps were already pounding up the stairs by the time they whipped across the landing and onto the iron ladder beyond the emergency exit.

The yellow pickup was parked by the ruined panel truck in the yard, and it took them less than a minute to reach it.

The pickup had a press-button starter with no ignition key. Bolan had floored the pedal and was steering out into the street before the first heads appeared, the first arms waving from the windows above. The only vehicle in sight was a rotary-brush road cleaner's cart drawn by two horses whose breath steamed in the freezing air. Bolan skated the pickup past and headed for the outskirts of town.

There was a left turn after the railroad bridge, and a sign pointing to Balta and Kotovsk. Bolan broadsided the Pobeda pickup onto the highway and trod on the gas pedal.

He had been right about the fresh snowfall. The road had been swept and gritted, but as far as they could see in every direction black leafless trees etched complex patterns into an undulating landscape of virgin white.

"I'm not complaining," Bolan said when the last houses were behind them, "but why did you do it? When you know I'm a phony, why take out the guy slated to get you away? Why knock off the regular contact to save *my* life?''

"I preferred to stay with you," said Ingrid.

He stared at her. She was looking ahead through the misted windshield, the wide mouth set in a slight smile. He frowned. It had been a great night but surely it was too much to expect that this alone would overturn a political belief, a fanatic conviction? "Why?" he asked again.

"He would have taken me to Albania. I do not want to go there."

The Pobeda swerved as Bolan's hands did a double take. "You don't want...but how else can you get to China?"

"I have no wish to go to China."

"Look," Bolan said quietly. "I tricked you, I deceived you, I took you away under false pretenses, okay. I am truly sorry for that. But you don't have to pretend—"

"None of those things matter," she interrupted. "I do not mind. In any case I too have been deceitful. I am not the person you believe me to be."

Icy fingers clutched Bolan's heart. Hell, he thought, they were wise to the deal and put in a ringer. After all he'd been through. Was this some eavesdropping lab assistant who latched onto the plan for her own reasons? Was this why she had been so reluctant to talk?

Seeing his expression she laughed. "Do not worry," she said. "I am still Ingrid Korsun."

"Professor of electronics at Kiev University?"

"Yes."

"Who designed and built the RIAMS computer?"

"Yes."

"And decided to transfer her work to China because communism in Russia had gone sour?"

"Who *said* that she had decided to do that," the woman corrected.

Momentarily he took his eyes from the road—they were twisting through a range of low wooded hills—to look at her again. "I don't understand."

"It is true that I am disenchanted with the situation in Russia—and remember that I am not Russian myself. But it is untrue that I believe things would be better in the People's Republic of China. I am cynical enough to imagine that the same kind of corruption will have rotted the ideal there too. It is a shaming thing," Ingrid said in a low voice, "but I wish to defect. . .and I wish to defect to the West. I believe my work would receive more encouragement and less hindrance there."

For some time Bolan was too stunned to reply. Then he said, "Are you telling me that this whole routine, the whole concept of smuggling yourself into Albania so that you could make Peking, was nothing but a blind?"

"Yes," she said. "That is what I am telling you."

"But why? Why go to all that length, make all those complicated and dangerous arrangements if you didn't intend to use them? Why not defect directly to the West?"

"To throw people off the scent. It is not such a crime to be *too* communist. And you must remember that I am. . .was. . .under surveillance. Because of the secret nature of my work I have never been permitted to attend any international conferences or contact my Western opposite numbers."

Bolan nodded. It was beginning to make sense.

"Under such conditions," Ingrid said, "it is extremely difficult for a nondiplomat to meet any Westerners at all. Even if you do, there is a risk that they will be afraid to help or that they themselves are being watched. As for our Russian dissidents, all of them are known to the authorities. Even to meet any of them would arouse suspicion."

"Yes," Bolan said, "I see that."

"It is relatively easy, on the other hand," she said, "to meet foreigners from other Eastern-bloc countries and through them the Albanians and Chinese, even if they are not well looked upon here. They are happy to have the opportunity to trick the Soviets. The important thing for me was to get out of Russia."

"And then?"

"I planned to let them take me as far as Albania and then bribe someone to ferry me across the sea to Italy. It is easier when one of the frontiers is a coastline."

For one or two miles they drove in silence. "There are many things I do not understand," Ingrid said at last. "That man Kriplin was right. You are the mystery. Nobody knows anything about you. Do you come from the West or the East? Who are you? Why are you here? Why did you take his place?"

Speaking carefully because the snow had begun to fall again and driving was becoming difficult, Bolan told her who he was and why he was there.

"But that is marvelous," she said when he had finished. "Paris, Rome, New York. The bright lights. It is all the same to me."

"More important than the bright lights," Bolan said soberly, "is something we like to call freedom."

"And you say that I shall have unlimited funds to develop my theories and build another RIAMS? Then Paris is the best of all. How do we get there from here?"

"A few miles ahead there is a town called Balta," Bolan said. "We will have to take the small roads and bypass that. Twenty-five miles farther on we come to Kotovsk on the border between the Ukraine and Moravia. Then we have to cross into Romania. Gypsy friends of those who sent me will pass us through to Yugoslavia. And from there we shall become winter vacationers and return to Italy the way you planned."

"You are a lovely man. How long will it take us?"

"It depends on the efficiency of the opposition. Major General Strakhov is a man of power. It may take several days and nights."

"Then I shall love you very well all of each night."

The thought was a great deal more welcome to Bolan now that he knew he would not have to cash in on it, to exploit the situation in order to upset the woman's convictions. "Then I'll be rooting for Strakhov," he said lightly.

There were frosted storks' nests on the roofs of Balta. It was not an easy town to bypass: the maze of lanes and minor roads that climbed north and west toward the high ground above the Dniester plain had not been cleared and at times the snow was deep. Bolan locked chains over the heavy-duty tires, but it was noon before they hit a signposted highway again, and then the road was icy.

There was little traffic.

Light faded as the snow fell more heavily. Once Bolan thought he heard a helicopter but it was impossible to see upward through the whirling flakes. He hoped it would be as difficult looking down through a Plexiglas blister.

By three o'clock, negotiating a hilly forest gashed by deep valleys and honeycombed with woodland trails, their pace had slowed to a crawl and the Pobeda was sliding dangerously on the snowpacked surface. When the wipers were no longer able to clear the glass quickly enough for Bolan to see, he pulled to the side and cut the engine.

He climbed out to stretch his legs. The snow was halfway to his knees. "If I read the map right," he said, "there's a pass no more than a couple, three hundred yards away. After that it's straight down to the plain. I'll take a look."

"You don't think they are following us?" she asked,

shivering a little as she pulled the *tchouba* tighter around her.

"I don't know. It's kind of crazy if they're not. I mean it doesn't take an Einstein to make a connection between the foreign man and woman who fled from a dead man in the hotel and the couple whose charred bodies were *not* found in the burned-out chopper yesterday. They'll certainly have the description of this pickup."

"Perhaps they do not know which way we went when we left Pervomaysk?"

"There's not all that much choice. And they've got enough manpower to cover every damned footpath in the state if they want." Bolan strained to look back along the sinuous route, hoping not to see the lights of any vehicle struggling toward them through the blizzard on some loop of road far below. If there was one it was invisible.

After the whine of gears and the racket of the engine it was frighteningly quiet. The snow fell silently from the sky. The wind that was piling it into drifts whispered through the branches of pines and firs ranked densely on either side of the road. Their voices were muffled.

Bolan strode ahead up the grade, his boots creaking on the fresh snow. The pass was in fact within 150 yards of the stalled pickup, around a sharp left-hand curve. There had been some drifting on the saddle but the trees there had sheltered most of the roadway. A couple of hours' work with the shovels in back of the Pobeda should clear them a passage. After that, once the snow stopped, it was plain sailing all the way.

They had been working for an hour when the snow stopped, revealing a sulfurous yellow sky laced with flying clouds that seemed no higher than the treetops. Despite the biting, bone-chilling cold, they were bathed in sweat by the time a channel wide enough for the pickup had been dug through the drift.

Bolan took powerful binoculars that Kriplin had left in the glove compartment and scanned the wintry panorama ahead.

The land fell away abruptly, earth and rock outcrops showing black through the snow where the slopes were in the lee of the wind. He followed the line of the road, now curving clearly, now invisible beneath a thick blanket of white. Five miles away he could see the intersection where they had to fork left for Kotovsk.

He could also see the barriers, the troop carriers, three GAZ 4x4 command trucks, the armored cars maneuvering for position. The tiny figures of officers directing the soldiers fanned out to block the country on either side of the road.

21

"We have to find some way around them. It's the only answer." Bolan picked up the Russian service revolver and the Walther he had snatched from Kriplin's body. "We can't take on that kind of force with two handguns and no spare ammunition."

"Wouldn't it be better to go back and try a different direction?" Ingrid said.

He shook his head. "The gas tank was only half full when we started. We've been driving in low most of the way. Pretty soon it will run dry. The last intersection we passed was more than five miles back. If we made it, we wouldn't have enough gas to go anyplace."

"And ahead?"

"They sure chose a good site. Between the saddle and their roadblock there isn't even the smell of a trail."

"But you said we had to make a detour."

"Sure I did. Without the pickup. I mean like on foot."

Bolan paused. He heard the noise first as an extension, almost imperceptible, of the winter silence surrounding them between the snow-covered walls of the pass—an intangible alteration and addition to the myriad small sounds of which that silence was composed: the sighing of wind, the stealthy patter of crystals falling from a tree branch, an indrawn breath, the tick of cooling metal from the engine.

Even when his ear had registered it as a separate sound, it was so unexpected in that place that at first he didn't believe it. But he was not mistaken. Somewhere not too far away there must be a railroad, because what he heard was the sound of a distant train laboring up a gradient.

He ran to the truck, folding back the pages of the map inside the cab. "Sure as hell," he exclaimed. "It's the branch linking Gayvoron with Podolskiy. There's a tunnel beneath the ridge. There must be a cut within a few hundred yards of this pass."

Sliding and staggering, they fought their way up the bank, through the trees and across an upland slope where the snow was waist deep. The train was nearer, the hoarse panting of a steam locomotive clearly audible somewhere behind and below them. At times the rhythm accelerated frantically as the drive wheels slipped on icy rails. "Sounds like a pretty steep grade," Bolan commented. "That means they'll be going slow when they reach the top."

The train, a six-car local, passed when they were still a hundred yards away. It entered the cut at a walking pace.

The single track ran between brick revetments for eighty yards before the tunnel mouth. Because there were overhanging trees, the ties were free of snow, though a light powdering dusted the cinder ballast between them. "Okay," Bolan said. "The first freight train and we hop a ride."

He went back for a final recon of the opposition. The binoculars showed him men working with shovels, clearing a deep drift at the foot of the hill. If Strakhov sent up half-tracks with orders to smell out the Pobeda pickup, they would have to pray for a fast freight arrival, for their tracks in the snow would betray them as surely as a pin on a wall map. The train had to be to hell and gone before the trackers radioed back to Strakhov with the news that they were on it. Otherwise he could have it stopped before they were clear.

A freight train passed twenty-five minutes later. It seemed a long wait to Bolan and the woman. Above the whine of the wind in the trees, he kept imagining he heard the shouts of pursuers arriving at the place where they had abandoned the pickup.

The train was hauled by an elderly tanker—two refrigerator cars, half a dozen flatbeds stacked with lumber, five loaded coal cars, three hoppers and two boxcars before the caboose.

Bolan and Ingrid were behind a snow-covered stack of replacement ties.

Breasting the rise, the tank locomotive jetted smoke and sparks into the sullen sky. The engineer was leaning out of his cab, staring ahead at the green light glowing by the arched tunnel mouth.

"Good thing these ties were on the other side of the track," Bolan said. "And pray again that the train carries no flagman, or if it does that he's keeping warm inside the caboose."

"They do not always have one crewing the smaller freights," Ingrid said.

The tanker's whistle shrilled. A plume of steam spurted as white as the snow against the dun-colored sky. Bolan heard a signal wire jerk over iced-up pulleys and then smoke flattened down and bellied out against the stonework as the locomotive entered the tunnel. The green light changed to red.

"Okay," he yelled, "make for the last flatcar and crawl under the tarp."

He figured the cars were passing at ten to fifteen miles per hour. They started running as the first refrigerator entered the tunnel. Alongside the sixth flatbed the woman leaped, caught hold of an iron stanchion, missed her footing and almost fell.

Bolan was near enough to grab her bodily and shove her up onto the car. But he himself was now dangerous-

ly near the tunnel, and there were no more cars behind
that he could jump.

He hurled himself at the flatcar's buffers, landed
among drawbars and couplings, pulled himself panting
up alongside the woman.

Seven minutes later they lifted a corner of the tarpaulin and saw the roadblock with its lines of soldiers
sliding past a mile away to the south.

"We should be okay at least until they stop the
train," Bolan told her. "You don't have cinder bulls in
this country. Because it's too risky, I guess, being a
hobo."

"Cinder bulls? Hobos?"

"Railroad police. They stop vagrants stealing free
rides the way we're doing now."

"Ah, the millions of capitalist unemployed that we
read about?"

"You shouldn't believe what you read, especially in
Russia. If you have no job in the West, you get relief,
unemployment pay," Bolan said. "In any case many of
the vagrants live that way because they want to: they are
free to choose."

"Free? That is the second time you say that. This
freedom of which you speak...."

"Put it this way," Bolan said. "Suppose the position
was reversed? Suppose you were a professor of electronics at UCLA or MIT and you wanted to go to Moscow. You wouldn't be lying under a tarp with a gun in
your hand, scared that you'd either be shot or sent to a
psychiatric prison in one of the gulags. You'd go to the
Soviet Embassy and get yourself a visa, and then you'd
simply pass by a travel agency and buy a ticket on whatever airline you chose. For that matter, if you wanted to
see a little of the world on the way, you could take the
boat and train. And the choice would be yours, not that
of some bureaucrat or local committee."

Ingrid fell silent, brooding deeply.

The train crossed a flat snowscape punctuated by grain silos and distant factory chimneys. Bolan looked at his watch. "They'll surely have discovered the pickup by now," he said. "And figured out from our tracks that we jumped either this train or the local before it. They're probably searching the local now. But it was almost a half hour ahead of us, so anytime this one stops we can reckon that search is completed, and we must be ready to fight."

"And if we get away?"

"We play it by ear," Bolan said. "So keep your fingers crossed. But only on one hand—you'll need the other one for this." He handed her the Russian service revolver.

Ten minutes later the train slowed. Buffers clattered as the brakes were applied. "This has to be the Moravia-Ukraine state line," Bolan said. "It's the obvious place. They'll have a checkpoint all ready for them."

He lifted the corner of the tarpaulin and peered out. The train was crawling around a long curve below an embankment. Above the white lip of the slope, a tiny airplane appeared. It was being thrown about the gray sky like a leaf in an autumn gale.

"Aerobatics," Bolan said. "Must be an airfield, maybe some kind of training school nearby. That's an old ship, piston-engined with a propeller."

The plane was a high-wing monoplane with a single tail-fin, a fixed spidery undercarriage, and a Plexiglas cabin. From time to time it sank from sight behind the steep embankment, then it would soar again, dipping and wheeling. Finally the pilot executed an immaculate loop, sideslipped to lose height and glided from sight in a shallow dive. The plane did not reappear.

"He's landed!" Bolan exclaimed. "The field must be just beyond this cut. Come on, this may be our last chance."

He threw back the tarp. The train was still slowing.

The place where the plane had disappeared was on the outside of the curve. Bolan climbed over the shrouded lumber to recon the inside.

As he expected, two hundred yards ahead of the locomotive a red light glowed. A line of soldiers was waiting between the track and a glassed-in cabin that looked like a control point.

Back on the outside, Bolan ordered: "Jump. They won't see us until we're near the top of the embankment above the level of the boxcar roofs."

They hit the ground and rolled, but the train was almost at a standstill now and it was no problem to scramble up and start plowing through the snow covering the bank.

Ten yards from the top, someone at the checkpoint got wise. There were shouts and pointed fingers and the crackle of automatic rifle fire. But Bolan and the woman were over the lip before the soldiers got the range right. The last the Executioner saw, two files of soldiers were running toward them along the track. The train squealed to a halt.

Beyond the embankment a wide snowfield stretched to a belt of trees. Half a mile away Bolan saw there were two canvas-covered hangars, a small hutted camp, a single tarmac runway. In front of the hangars two more monoplanes stood like outsize mosquitoes among Tupolev trainers, an old Dornier transport and an army version of the twin-jet Ilyushin executive.

Bolan took in the scene at a glance.

There were army vehicles in front of the huts and soldiers near the aircraft, but no jet fighters, bombers or other warplanes on the apron. Two sentries stood outside a striped box next to the wooden entrance gates.

The perimeter track was bordered by a simple wire fence, and the runway joined it less than a hundred yards from the top of the embankment. Between the two, another couple of sentries paced beneath a line of bare lime trees. The men were wearing long army great-coats with fur hats and slung Makarov machine pistols. It was clear that they had not yet heard the hubbub in the cut below.

Beyond the trees beside a wind sock on a mast, the aircraft that had just landed was visible. It was standing with its engine idling, evidently awaiting a signal to take off again.

The plane was a German-built Feiseler Fi-156 Storch, an artillery spotter that had been in service in several countries for forty years. With a forty-five-foot wing-span, a motor of only 240hp and a weight of less than a ton and a half, the Storch's top speed was no more than ninety miles per hour. Downwind the machine would just make the ton, and on a windless day it could fly as slow as thirty miles per hour.

What was more important to Bolan was that the Fi-156 could take off or land in a short distance.

That was the factor he counted on to save them.

Crouched on the lip of the embankment, neither he nor the woman had been noticed yet by the two guards. Bolan fitted the silencer to the Walther.

When the men were one hundred feet away, he raised the gun. The small sound marking the explosive charge was inaudible over the rumble of the aircraft engine and the panting of the stalled locomotive in the cutting below.

The nearer of the guards bucked sideways and flattened the snow as the slug smashed his skull.

His companion swung around, startled out of his wits by the silent deathblow. Unslinging his gun he saw two figures, widely separated, each with a weapon.

"Run away from me. Fire one shot," Bolan had instructed before the Walther sneezed out its fatal message. "You won't hit him but it will draw his fire."

He had guessed right. The crack of Ingrid's revolver rang out over the snow. The soldier, faced with two armed adversaries, instinctively aimed first at the one making the noise, the one whose gun was spitting fire.

Unlike Mack Bolan he guessed wrong. The second shot from the silenced Walther took him in the throat as he pressed the trigger of his machine pistol. The fountain of blood that sprayed upward while he fell rivaled the single short burst that hosed lead uselessly at the sky.

Bolan was running for the plane. Ingrid raced after him.

Bolan picked up the first soldier's Makarov without breaking his stride and vaulted the wire fence. The pilot of the plane was feeding the engine short bursts of throttle. He had neither heard nor seen anything yet.

The Storch swung around into the wind.

The pilot glanced sideways, and saw a big guy in a fleece-lined coat hanging one-handed to the starboard V-shaped strut that supported the top wing. There was a machine pistol in his free hand.

The flier reached for the Tokarev pistol holstered beneath his flying jacket. The big guy raised his gun hand.

In the last hundredth of a second the pilot saw the round black hole of the Makarov's muzzle veiled by a tiny point of fire. The fire brightened and spread unbelievably fast. Blazing furiously it flamed out searing fingers and snatched apart the Plexiglas cabin window. Once inside it expanded with white-hot speed and engulfed the world.

Bolan jerked open the door and pulled the body to the ground. He pushed Ingrid up into the passenger seat and slid behind the controls. He flipped off the brakes and slammed open the throttle. The tiny plane surged forward.

Five hundred yards away outside the hangars, Red

Army men were shouting. Two steel-helmeted guards piled into a turretless GAZ scout car and raced toward the runway. The sentries at the gate ran to a sandbagged machine gun emplacement.

Bolan was hitting fifty miles per hour when the GAZ was four hundred yards away, but he couldn't head directly for the car. The machine gun in the rear, aimed by the man behind the driver, was already spitting fire and a single bullet touching the prop would mean the end.

But the Storch was not going fast enough to lift off before they were within accurate range of the gun.

Bolan guided the machine off the runway, kicking the rudder hard left, and bumped across the snow-covered grass, outflanking the scout car.

The GAZ skidded to a halt, wheeled around and resumed the chase. Only now it was a stern chase, and although its speed had been cut down off the runway, the Feiseler started gaining as soon as it was back on the tarmac.

The panning machine gun at the gate fired as the plane roared past. Slugs punctured the back of the fuselage; two of the greenhouse side panels starred. There were holes in the starboard wing.

Bolan shouted to Ingrid to lie down behind the tandem seats. He kept one hand on the control column and picked up the Makarov. Spraying lead one-handed through the still-open door, he saw a machine gunner slump over the sandbags. Men running for one of the aircraft on the apron threw themselves flat. An officer aiming a submachine gun at the Storch crumpled to the ground.

Then the plane was beyond the hangars, still gaining speed . . . and lifting. The runway was sixty feet beneath them before they had covered half its length.

Bolan pulled the door shut against the freezing airstream and laughed aloud.

Ingrid picked herself up and moved back to the passenger seat beside him. "I think you are wonderful," she said. "Where do you fly this machine now?"

"We're going to meet the Gypsies."

"Will they not follow and shoot us down with other planes from that field? We fly very slowly."

He shook his head. "That's a primary training field. None of those ships are armed. By the time they call up the jets we'll be into the Carpathian foothills and long gone, even at this speed."

"How far is it?"

"Fifteen, twenty miles. We're way below their radar again. And the ground-to-air defenses between Warsaw Pact countries are not all that sophisticated. In any case, once we hit those hills we'll be hedgehopping, flying along each valley below the crests. Nobody's going to know we're there until we've gone!"

The wind was shrieking through the bullet holes in the canopy, knifing cold air into the cabin through the rips in the fuselage fabric. They flew at three hundred feet across the Dniester plain, passed over the frozen loops of the river and headed northwest for the frontier.

Ingrid leaned her head on his shoulder. "When this darkness is over," she said, "before I start to work in Paris, you will show me the bright lights, yes?"

"As bright as they come, baby."

For the moment Bolan was content. Mission accomplished. Yeah.

But there were seven hundred thousand KGB agents at large in the world, each one a sucker on the numberless tentacles of the octopus conspiracy that threatened to stifle the good things in a wearied Western civilization.

In the past few days Bolan had accounted for some, wasted a few of the soldiers who supported them and succeeded in withdrawing from their grasp one of the best intel experts in the business.

It was only a small step—small compared with the endless magnitude of his self-imposed task—but it was positive. It was a step that would in time help greatly in the evaluation of the enemy plots and plans. And although the physical losses inflicted had been minimal, a more important moral victory had been won.

For Strakhov and his minions had lost face. Their prey had been within their grasp and they had let him escape. He had dared to penetrate their stronghold and make off with a prize. And he had got away with it.

In psychological terms that victory was worth a lot of soldiers.

But so far as Bolan was concerned, he had simply won a minor skirmish. Not a battle and certainly not the war. There were seven hundred thousand reasons why this trip in the Storch was no one-way joyride—and each one of them had a description of Bolan and an order to kill him on sight.

Yeah, those were the odds, but this was a fight he was ready for. Paris and the bright lights were just a breather in his corner before he came out fighting for the next round.

They had just about time to overfly the border and put down near the waiting Gypsies at Solca before the jets with their rockets caught up with them.

In the gathering dusk the tiny monoplane flew up the first of the Carpathian valleys and was lost to sight against the forest trees.

MORE ADVENTURE NEXT MONTH WITH

MACK BOLAN

#71 Blood Dues

New Miami war!

Rumors and rumbles of a Cuban exile connection with the Mafia crime machine in Miami have come to Bolan's ears.

The Executioner enters an old battleground, only to find hordes of Cuban outcasts crowding the city center, and the teeming core of Miami pulsing to a new Latin death song.

Grim specters and faithful friends of a former life weave a déjà vu tapestry as Bolan hits both the Mob and an exile splinter movement.

Clouds of terror hang low over America's southern ocean playground. The rumbles are turning to thunder. Unless Bolan can stop the Havana hurricane, Miami and its beaches will be awash with blood!

DON PENDLETON'S EXECUTIONER

MACK BOLAN

Sergeant Mercy in Nam...The Executioner in the Mafia Wars...Colonel John Phoenix in the Terrorist Wars.... Now Mack Bolan fights his loneliest war! You've never read writing like this before. Faceless dogsoldiers have killed April Rose. The Executioner's one link with compassion is broken. His path is clear: by fire and maneuver, he will rack up hell in a world shock-tilted by terror. Bolan wages unsanctioned war—everywhere!

GOLD EAGLE

Available wherever paperbacks are sold.

**You've not read action–adventure
until you've read**

**Day of Mourning
Terminal Velocity
Dead Man Running**

*These are the three Mack Bolan books in which he
began his incredible new career. No action-adventure
reading is complete without this trilogy. Enjoy your
greatest action experience ever in three linked stories
that hurl the lethal human javelin known as
The Executioner into the heart of world terror.*

A wanton assault on Mack Bolan's command base leaves
his one true love, April Rose, slain.

Fueled by white-hot rage and thoughts of wild revenge,
The Executioner pursues his sacred quest to Moscow,
lair of the sinister spearhead.

Bolan fingers the perpetrator in Russia and follows the
trail of treachery back to the U.S. He rains a hellstorm
of death on Washington, the city of lies, and comes face
to face with the traitor at last—in the Oval Office itself!

"The best of the best." —*Florida Constitution*

HE'S EXPLOSIVE. HE'S MACK BOLAN... AGAINST ALL ODDS

He learned his deadly skills in Vietnam...then put them to good use by destroying the Mafia in a blazing one-man war. Now **Mack Bolan** ventures further into the cold to take on his deadliest challenge yet— the KGB's worldwide terror machine.

Follow the lone warrior on his exciting new missions...and get ready for more nonstop action from his high-powered combat teams: **Able Team**—Bolan's famous Death Squad—battling urban savagery too brutal and volatile for regular law enforcement. And **Phoenix Force**—five extraordinary warriors handpicked by Bolan to fight the dirtiest of antiterrorist wars, blazing into even greater danger.

Fight alongside these three courageous forces for freedom in all-new action-packed novels! Travel to the gloomy depths of the cold Atlantic, the scorching sands of the Sahara, and the desolate Russian plains. You'll feel the pressure and excitement building page after page, with nonstop action that keeps you enthralled until the explosive conclusion!

Now you can have all the new Gold Eagle novels delivered right to your home!

You won't want to miss a single one of these exciting new action-adventures. And you don't have to! Just fill out and mail the card at right, and we'll enter your name in the Gold Eagle home subscription plan. You'll then receive six brand-new action-packed Gold Eagle books every other month, delivered right to your home! You'll get two Mack Bolan novels, one Able Team and one Phoenix Force, plus one book each from two thrilling, new Gold Eagle libraries, **SOBs** and **Track**. In **SOBs** you'll meet the legendary team of mercenary warriors who fight for justice and win. **Track** features a military and weapons genius on a mission to stop a maniac whose dream is everybody's worst nightmare. Only Track stands between us and nuclear hell!

FREE! The New War Book and Mack Bolan bumper sticker.

As soon as we receive your card we'll rush you the long-awaited New War Book and Mack Bolan bumper sticker—both ABSOLUTELY FREE. Then under separate cover, you'll receive your six Gold Eagle novels.

The New War Book is *packed* with exciting information for Bolan fans: a revealing look at the hero's life...two new short stories...book character biographies...even a combat catalog describing weapons used in the novels! The New War Book is a special collector's item you'll want to read again and again. And it's yours FREE when you mail your card!

Of course, you're under no obligation to buy anything. Your first six books come on a 10-day free trial—if you're not thrilled with them, just return them and owe nothing. The New War Book and bumper sticker are yours to keep, FREE!

Don't miss a single one of these thrilling novels...mail the card now, while you're thinking about it.

HE'S UNSTOPPABLE. AND HE'LL FIGHT TO DEFEND FREEDOM!

Mail this coupon today!

1. How do you rate _____ ?
   (Please print book TITLE)

   1.6 ☐ excellent   .4 ☐ good   .2 ☐ not so good

   .5 ☐ very good   .3 ☐ fair   .1 ☐ poor

2. How likely are you to purchase another book in this series?

   2.1 ☐ definitely would purchase   .3 ☐ probably would not purchase

   .2 ☐ probably would purchase   .4 ☐ definitely would not purchase

3. How do you compare this book with similar books you usually read?

   3.1 ☐ far better than others   .4 ☐ not as good

   .2 ☐ better than others   .5 ☐ definitely not as good

   .3 ☐ about the same

4. Have you any additional comments about this book?

   _____ (4)

   _____ (6)

5. How did you *first* become aware of this book?

   8. ☐ read other books in series   11. ☐ friend's recommendation

   9. ☐ in-store display   12. ☐ ad inside other books

   10. ☐ TV, radio or magazine ad   13. ☐ other _____
   (please specify)

6. What *most* prompted you to buy this book?

   14. ☐ read other books in series   17. ☐ title   20. ☐ story outline on back

   15. ☐ friend's recommendation   18. ☐ author   21. ☐ read a few pages

   16. ☐ picture on cover   19. ☐ advertising   22. ☐ other _____
   (please specify)

7. Have you purchased any books from any of these series or by these authors in the past 12 months? Approximately how many?

	No. Purchased		No. Purchased
☐ Mack Bolan	(23) _____	☐ Clive Cussler	(49) _____
☐ Able Team	(25) _____	☐ Len Deighton	(51) _____
☐ Phoenix Force	(27) _____	☐ Ken Follet	(53) _____
☐ SOBs	(29) _____	☐ Colin Forbes	(55) _____
☐ Dagger	(31) _____	☐ Frederick Forsyth	(57) _____
☐ The Destroyer	(33) _____	☐ Adam Hall	(59) _____
☐ Death Merchant	(35) _____	☐ Jack Higgins	(61) _____
☐ The Mercenary	(37) _____	☐ Gregory MacDonald	(63) _____
☐ Casca	(39) _____	☐ John D. MacDonald	(65) _____
☐ Nick Carter	(41) _____	☐ Robert Ludlum	(67) _____
☐ The Survivalist	(43) _____	☐ Alistair MacLean	(69) _____
☐ Duncan Kyle	(45) _____	☐ John Gardner	(71) _____
☐ Stephen King	(47) _____	☐ Helen McInnes	(72) _____

8. On which date was this book purchased? (75) _____

9. Please indicate your age group and sex.

   77.1 ☐ Male   78.1 ☐ under 15   .3 ☐ 25-34   .5 ☐ 50-64

   .2 ☐ Female   .2 ☐ 15-24   .4 ☐ 35-49   .6 ☐ 65 or older

Thank you for completing and returning this questionnaire.

X12345

NAME _____

ADDRESS _____

(Please Print)

CITY _____

ZIP CODE _____

BUSINESS REPLY MAIL

FIRST CLASS   PERMIT NO. 70   TEMPE, AZ.

POSTAGE WILL BE PAID BY ADDRESSEE

NATIONAL READER SURVEYS

2504 West Southern Avenue
Tempe, AZ   85282